Michael Freemantle

The Long Purr

a tale of two strays

Typeset in Minion Pro

Design, typesetting and publishing by UK Book Publishing

www.ukbookpublishing.com

ISBN: 978-1-914195-39-6

DISCLAIMER

No cats were harmed or destroyed in pawing this book or in the research carried out for it. All the cats portrayed in the book are fictitious. Any resemblance to real cats living or dead is coincidental and not intended to cause offence. Views and opinions expressed by the cats in this book are not necessarily those of the author. The text has been scrupulously checked for accuracy and every non-cat word spell-checked on a computer belonging to the author's mistress. The author takes full responsibility for any errors that may have crept into the text undercover while she was dreaming.

The Long Purr

a tale of two strays

an entertainment for cat lovers

pawed by Clawdia

Chapter One

THE HAPLESS CAT INN

I, Clawdia, had a dream, a long dream:

Not so long ago, two cats met under a hedge at the Hapless Cat Inn in the village of Slithadown. It was a popular spot for hapless cats. Happy customers leaving the pub often dropped bread crusts, slivers of sandwiches, juicy pieces of salmon or salami, fragments of crisps, and crumbs of crunchy biscuits in the car park. And at weekends, when the weather was warm and fine, children scattered scraps of food under and around the tables in the beer garden.

Pigeons, sparrows, starlings, magpies, mice, rats, foxes, hedgehogs, and runaway dogs loved to visit the garden for picnics when the humans had left. But cats, especially those with piercing eyes, sharp teeth, and powerful hisses traditionally had scrap-picking priority.

On this not-so-long-ago pre-Covid day, the two cats eyed each other suspiciously under the hedge at the side of the garden. Noisy children played at a nearby table while their parents chatted and drank beer and wine. The unseasonably warm late-March weather had brought human weekenders out in droves to the garden.

One of the cats was orange with white paws and deep blue eyes. He looked tearful. The other was black with sparkling green eyes.

'Have you come far?' she asked in a queenly sort of way.

'I'm a stray,' said the orange cat. 'I've been straying around here since I was a kitten.'

'I'm also a stray,' said the black cat lifting her head to reveal a pale blue collar around her neck. 'It's an intercounty stray collar – but I forgot to reactivate it when it expired, so it doesn't work.'

The orange cat suspected that he should know about intercounty stray collars but was not sure what to say. He stared at the collar for several minutes, scratched his head, and shifted uncomfortably.

'What are intercounty stray collars?' he asked eventually.

'They allow you to go anywhere and everywhere within reason,' she answered without fur-ther explanation. 'I come here every Saturday evening and

Sunday afternoon when I'm hungry and the weather is fine.'

'I like the cat-ering here,' she continued. 'The battered fish and triple-cooked chips, when you can get them, are particularly tasty. I can also recommend the chicken burgers.'

The orange cat explained that, although he was local, he had always been afraid to visit the inn even though it cat-ered well for cats. He said his name was Clem.

'My name is Jet,' said the black stray holding out a front paw for a pawshake.

A half-eaten tuna sandwich came flying towards them followed by a nibbled-at chicken leg. The two cats carefully sniffed the food and slowly dragged it under the hedge. They decided to share the feast. Afterwards, they wandered off to the car park and snoozed blissfully beneath the engine of a large silver Mercedes estate car.

'You look sad,' said Jet when they woke up.

'I miss my sister Catrina,' sobbed Clem. 'She's a year older than me but ran away when I was young. I've looked everywhere but cannot find her. You should have seen her. She was beautiful and brave. She could scare off dogs and foxes. Now I'm so lonely.'

Jet looked puzzled. 'Catrina? I don't think I've seen her.'

Clem explained that he used to live in a mews house with his mother and sister. The residents, a man and a woman, loved them and fed them twice a day. One day, after they had gone to work, there was a flash flood.

'Catrina, Ma-puss, and I were resting on a mat near the oven in the kitchen when the water began seeping through the kitchen door. Ma-puss clasped me by the scruff of my neck, splashed through the water, and struggled with me upstairs. She then went back to fetch Catrina but could not find her in any of the rooms on the ground floor.'

Jet listened attentively, fascinated by his story. 'What happened next?'

'All the time, the water was rising,' Clem continued. 'Ma-puss did not come back upstairs. I was frightened. After waiting several hours for the water to go away, I went downstairs looking for something to eat. I saw Ma-puss stretched out at the foot of the stairs covered in mud. She had drowned as the waters rose. Catrina was nowhere to be seen. She must have escaped through an open window. When the humans came back, I darted out through the door to look for Catrina.'

'And you couldn't find her?'

'No, I've been searching for her ever since.'

'Did you go back to the house?'

'No, I was afraid to.'

'How sad!' said Jet sympathetically. 'You poor poor thing. Where do you think she's gone?'

'I think she may have headed south to the sea. The humans always talked about going south to the sea for a picnic or barbeque. I tried to follow Catrina but soon lost her scent. So I came back to Slithadown and wandered around.'

'Wouldn't it be great if we looked for Catrina together,' suggested Jet. 'What do you think?'

'Cats that stray together stay together.'

'We can head south to the sea like Catrina. I know lots of cats and eating places south of here. But first we need to cheer you up. And then you must learn a few things about straying and searching, because straying and searching can be tough for a novice cat like you.'

Jet picked up a piece of chicken from a discarded burger. Clem grabbed a half-eaten sausage and the two hapless cats set off.

Chapter Two

DRAWING OUT THE SADNESS

Jet and Clem wandered side by side down a narrow lane from the Hapless Cat Inn diving into a ditch whenever a car, van, or bicycle approached. They stopped on a grass verge to eat the chicken together.

'Hold on to the sausage,' said Jet. 'We'll need it.'

'Are we heading south to the sea?' asked Clem after chewing the last morsel of chicken.

Jet raised her head towards the sky. 'The sun rises in the east and sets in the west,' she said. 'South is in between and north behind us.'

Clem nodded pretending to understand.

'I have a sister, a twin sister,' said Jet, changing the subject.

'You didn't tell me.'

'You didn't ask.'

'What's her name?'

'Clawdia. She is intelligent, beautiful, and fluent in spoken and written English. She understands humans purr-fectly and is a brilliant writer. She sleeps in luxury and loves to dream. She was a TV star once – she appeared regularly on *One Woman and Her Cat*.'

'Where does she live?'

'In Uppandown with Mistress Maud. She has a gloriously warm house with deep rugs and lots of soft cushions. Mistress Maud is rich. She adopted Clawdia when we were kittens just a few months old.'

'And not you?'

'No one wanted me. My master tried to drown me in a bucket of water, but I bit one of his fingers and escaped. I hid under a large rhododendron bush in his garden, curled up, and went to sleep. When I woke up, it was dark, and I was all alone. I've been straying ever since.'

'Where did you get your collar?'

Before Jet could answer, he thought of another question. 'Aren't you jealous of Clawdia?'

'Oh no!' Jet exclaimed. 'She is good to me. I visit her quite often – but I have to get there early in the morning when she does her garden round. Mistress Maud shoos me away if she sees me. We've spent hours out of her sight chatting and chasing birds and squirrels in the garden. When I see Clawdia, we cat-ch up with all the mews on the cat-vine. Feline friends flock from miles around in the summer to nip the catmint in her garden. They say it's the best catmint in all the down villages. She jokes that if she had a penny for every one of their nips, she'd be a millionaire. But who needs money when you can live in luxury?'

'How did she learn English?'

'When her mistress is home, they spend hours watching television. Clawdia sits on her lap and they watch programmes about geography, the countryside, history, and lots of other things. Her son Frank visits her every other day. Her next-door neighbour Marjory is a scientist but she finds her boring with all that scientific talk. The local vicar also calls on her from time to time. Clawdia is always quick on the uptake. She loves to jump on and off her mistress's knee to listen and learn. And sometimes she follows Mistress Maud to church on Sundays. If Mistress Maud had chosen me, I could have lived there instead. Clawdia understands that well and tells me she's blessed. "There but for the grace of God, it's me and not you," she always says.'

Clem was beginning to wish he hadn't asked Jet about her sister. He didn't want her to forget that he also had a sister and searching for her was the reason they were together.

'Do you think we'll find Catrina soon?' he asked.

'We'll have to be patient and keep our eyes open, nostrils flared, and whiskers clean. What did she look like? Ginger like you?'

Clem was pleased he had drawn her attention back to Catrina but looked at her with a puzzled expression. 'Do you mean orange like me?' he asked with just a hint of annoyance.

Jet smiled. 'Sorry! What did she look like? Orange like you?'

'Our Ma-puss was orange like me,' replied Clem. 'She told me that my Pa-puss was also orange like me but Catrina's Pa-puss was black and white.'

Clem was silent for a moment. He was thinking of telling Jet how proud he was to be an orange cat and how he thanked his mother for that. He would like to have thanked his father as well but never had the chance. He had never met him.

'You didn't answer my question,' said Jet. 'Was Catrina orange and did she have white paws and blue eyes, like yours?

'She has blue eyes like me but large patches of white all over her body as well as some orange and black.'

'Multicoloured, then?'

'Tricoloured.'

'A calico, then.'

Clem nodded although he was not familiar with the word 'calico.'

After they had finished the chicken, they headed along the lane again. Clem clutched the sausage in his mouth. Tears began to well in his eyes at the thought of his lost sister.

Jet cast him a glance, grimaced, and continued walking without a word. She stopped at a track that led from the lane through an open gate to a tumble-down wooden barn in the middle of an overgrown field. 'Before we go further, we need to draw the sadness out of you.'

Clem felt somewhat uneasy at the prospect. He wasn't sure what she intended. But he could not say a word: he still had the sausage in his mouth and found it difficult to talk. In any case, he was beginning to have confidence in Jet. She seemed to have all the answers and knew where they were and what they were doing. Like her sister, she was intelligent.

'This is Feelindown Barn where the Purr-haps family live,' Jet explained. 'There are lots of Purr-haps pussies here, but we have to be careful. Some are friendly and some not.'

A tubby tabby with bulging muscles and a scar above his eyes appeared from a gap beneath the barn door.

'Yeh?' he hissed threateningly.

'Is Purr-ceive in?' asked Jet in her best polite voice.

The tubby tabby turned towards the barn and shouted: 'Purr-ceive! One of the all blacks has come to see yuh.' He then disappeared.

'Come in if you're good looking,' shouted a voice from within.

Jet glanced at Clem with a glint in her eye. As they entered the barn, their noses twitched at the smell of stale straw, rotting wood, old sacks, damp newspapers, and mould. Through the gloom of the barn they noticed a shabby tabby hunched on a sack next to a bale of straw. It was Purr-ceive. Her eyes lit up when she saw Jet.

'I have brought you a client,' said Jet as she greeted Purr-ceive. 'His name is Clem and he has come for sadness therapy. I want you to draw the sadness out of him.'

'What an unhappy looking cat,' said Purr-ceive. 'But I see he is kind. He has brought me a nice piece of sausage. So, he needs a bit of cat-harsis does he? I'll see what we can do.'

Clem lay the sausage at Purr-ceive's paws. The shabby tabby gobbled it up and then pointed to the bale of straw. Clem sprang onto it and stared at the shabby tabby.

'Why are you sad?' asked Purr-ceive getting straight to the point.

'I'm looking for my sister Catrina – you should have seen her.'

'The cat spat on the mat,' interrupted Purr-ceive licking a morsel of sausage from her paw. 'Now close your eyes and say what I've just said.'

Clem closed his eyes. 'Say what I've just said,' he mumbled anxiously.

'No, not that. Say what I said before that.'

'Now close your eyes.'

'No, no, no!' said the shabby tabby grimly.

Jet whispered into Clem's ear. 'The cat …"

'The cat spat on the mat,' said Clem finally.

'Good,' said Purr-ceive. 'Now, repeat after me: the fox caught chicken pox from the ox.'

'The fox caught the chicken and the ox,' said Clem.

Purr-ceive wandered over to Jet for a private consultation and waved her paws forlornly. She tip-pawed off to another corner of the barn muttering that she would have to try something different. All was quiet for minute and then the two strays heard an excited miaow.

A sprightly young tabby appeared carrying a long piece of string that disappeared beneath a pile of sacks. 'My name is Purr-key and I've come to cheer you up. This string will draw the sadness out of you. Go and slouch on the couch.'

The young tabby waved a paw at a pile of sacks which Clem took to be the couch. As soon as Clem jumped onto the pile, Purr-key pulled the string. A grubby clockwork toy mouse on wheels shot out from beneath the sacks. Clem instinctively raced after the toy.

Jet, Purr-ceive, and Purr-key laughed as they watched. Clem caught and pawed the toy playfully. The string was tied to a rusty wind-up key attached to the toy. As he skipped around the toy patting and pawing it tentatively, Clem became aware of another cat emerging from the gloom at the other end of the barn. He looked over his shoulder to see a teenage tabby with pointed ears, angry eyes, and fang-like teeth staring at him.

'It's Purr-sue,' cried Jet, alarmed. 'Quick! We need to run for our lives.'

The two cats raced out of the barn pursued by Purr-sue. Never in their lives had they run so fast. They sped through a copse scattering squawking pheasants, crossed a recently ploughed field, and darted through a hedge avoiding the nettles and brambles.

They stopped and looked round. Purr-sue had given up the chase and turned back to the barn. The two strays scrambled over a fence and headed along a road towards the entrance to a farm.

'We've lost Purr-sue,' said Jet breathlessly.

It started to rain.

'Are we still going south?' asked Clem anxiously. 'I can't see the sun.'

Jet didn't answer. Clem looked at the sign on the gate but said not a word. 'Settuldown Farm,' said Jet glancing at the sign.

They squeezed through the gate and paw-sed next to a shed with an open door. They peeped inside and could just make out a wheelbarrow filled with hessian sacks. As their eyes became accustomed to the dim light, they noticed an old tractor and some movement beneath it.

An ageing grey cat covered in grime emerged. He wiped his brow with a greasy rag and held out a grubby right paw for a pawshake to greet the two hapless cats.

'It's Truffle Le Tracteur, isn't it?' asked Jet.

'You have a good memory for a pawsome face,' he replied turning his attention to Clem. 'We were just young kittens when we last met. Welcome to Settuldown Farm.'

'My name's Clem,' said Clem withdrawing his paw from the pawshake. He licked it to remove a spot of oil.

'This is where I live – under this beauty,' explained Truffle Le Tracteur.

He pointed a paw at the tractor.

'It's a Messy Fur-guson, a five-cylinder job. Classic vintage if you ask me.'

'We weren't asking, and don't get technical with us,' replied Jet cheekily.

The rain started to pour in torrents splashing up farmyard mud outside the shed.

'Hop into the wheelbarrow and hide under the sacks.' shouted the old grey cat. 'You can settle down there for the night if you like.'

He disappeared back under the tractor.

'Hop? Who does he think we are, bunny rabbits?' asked Jet as they snuggled under the sacks. Clem smiled.

The two exhausted cats went to sleep.

Chapter Three

ON THE FARM

Early the following morning, Clem poked his head out from the sacks. It was still raining. Two border collies sheltered inside the door unaware of his gaze. One was black and white, the other brown and white.

'It's raining cats and dogs,' said the black and white collie. She grinned as if she knew this would infuriate the other collie.

'Rosie, my friend! You know that always makes me mad,' said the brown and white collie. 'Cats get the credit for everything. They always get priority.'

'You do go on and on about it, Toby,' said Rosie. 'It makes no difference to me.'

'It should be "dogs and cats" not "cats and dogs," my friend,' said Toby. 'All cats do is sleep, sup the creamiest milk, and then catch a sparrow or mouse or two when they feel like it. It's not fair, my friend. And when you think about what we do. We round up sheep all day long and obey the master's every beck and whistle.'

'The master is proud of us,' said Rosie.

'Bah!' muttered Toby. 'You suck up to him, my friend. You gaze admiringly into his eyes and hang out your tongue panting just to flatter him. His wife calls you "the cat's whiskers." How annoying, she should say "you're the dog's whiskers." It's obvious.'

The two collies pawsed to pant for a while and look out to see if the rain had stopped. It hadn't.

'I know what you're going to complain about next. Go on: the cat ...,' said Rosie knowingly

'That so annoys me, my friend,' said Toby. 'Why does the master always have to say: "that will put the cat among the pigeons"? Why can't he say: "that will put the dog amock in the flock"? And why, when he comes into the shed, does he say, "you couldn't swing a cat in here"? Why can't he say "you couldn't swing a terrier in here"?'

'A terrier in the interior,' retorted Rosie grinning.

'And when he throws a ball up in the air, he doesn't say: "dog-get it!" does he?' continued Toby doggedly. 'He says: "cat-ch it!" What have cats got to do with it, my friend? Look at that field on the hill. It should be full of dog-tle. But no! It's full of cat-tle. Why call them that? Just because cats drink cat-tle milk? The only time humans use our name is when things turn nasty. "Oh look! He's made a real dog's dinner of that," or "it's a dog's life." And then we have those silly rhymes called doggerel.'

The rain stopped. Two red kites with their forked tails swept over the farmyard. One screeched fearfully as the other pursued swooping and turning acrobatically. Two mobbing crows flew up from a field to join the action above the farmyard. They chased the kites away.

'That looked like a dog fight!' joked Rosie. 'Now that it's raining cats and dogs, we'd better be off. We must go and see Sally.'

'OK, my friend, I've heard that one before,' barked Toby. 'We have to sally forth.'

'And we have to see a dog about a man.'

Toby cast Rosie a critical look as they walked away.

'Did you hear all that?' Clem asked Jet who had now woken up. 'Was that what humans called dogma or a dog in the manger?'

Before Jet could answer Truffle Le Tracteur appeared from under the tractor. He was yawning. 'You'd better be on your way without delay. The master will soon be on the heels of Rosie and Toby. I know him well.'

The two hapless cats jumped down from the wheelbarrow, hastily bid him goodbye, and tentatively emerged from the shed. They turned in unison to see the master in muddy Wellington boots striding towards the two collies who were waiting at the gate on the other side of the farmyard. The farmer immediately saw the two hapless cats.

'A nice little 'arvest we 'av 'ere!' he shouted in a throaty southern dialect. A small pebble whizzed past their ears. Jet looked around to see him pulling back a piece of elastic from a Y-shaped wooden frame.

'I'll 'av yer fur for fur-tiliser,' he added laughing as another pebble whistled over their heads and splashed into a puddle in front of them.

The two cats jumped over the puddle and sprinted through the farmyard towards the gate leaving the chuckling farmer and the Settuldown Farm barns and sheds well behind. The two collies, who were now arguing with each other angrily, ignored them. Only when the two strays were well along the road did the strays stop to hide under a laurel bush.

'He had a wooden slingshot cat-apult,' said Jet casting a fur-tive glance behind her. 'Our Albanian ancestors invented apult weapons thousands of years ago for killing rats and scaring pigeons. That was before humans copied our invention.'

Clem was astounded at Jet's knowledge of such things. The two cats rested as the sky brightened.

'Now we'll go on our way to find Catrina,' said Jet. 'But first we need to get you registered as a stray'

'Registered?'

'Yes, registered. You're a local stray. If your mother had lived, she would have told you that you cannot stray over other cats' territories without being registered at the lost strays' office. You need an intercounty stray purr-mit.'

She pointed to her blue collar. 'This is my purr-mit, but it's lost its smell – so I need to reactivate it with a legitimate intercounty scent mark. I can go anywhere with it when it's activated. See that hill over there and the woods? There's a cottage on the other side. That's where the office is. I will vouch for your stray status. Every cat in charge of a registered territory recognises an activated intercounty stray purr-mit.'

Chapter Four

THE INTERCOUNTY STRAYS' OFFICE

The late-March sun appeared again and by early afternoon the two strays arrived hot, hungry, and tired at a picnic area on the edge of a copse of beech and oak trees. Rowdy human teenagers on a school outing were clambering into a minibus. Jet and Clem waited until they disappeared. There were no other picnickers. The wooden benches were empty but the litter bins were overflowing with discarded cans, plastic bottles, empty packaging, and an assortment of unrecognisable debris.

'Do you fancy a spot of lunch?' said Jet.

The two hapless cats foraged around the area. Clem could not find a crust of food. 'The foxes must have got here first,' he said, although there was not a whiff of another animal.

Jet spied a wrapper containing an uneaten baguette filled with ham and tomato. She pushed it under the nearest bench. The two cats settled down to enjoy the meal, sharing the thin slices of ham between them.

'We'd better move on before it gets dark,' said Jet when they had finished eating.

They followed a pawpath through the trees for about an hour until it merged with a human footpath. The footpath then divided into two at a wooden fingerpost. One finger read: 'South to the Sea,' the other: 'To the Cottage.'

'Which way do we go?' asked Clem ignoring the signs.

Jet stared at Clem in puzzlement. She then realised to her astonishment that Clem could not read. She decided not to mention it.

'We'd better stay here for the night,' she said. 'It'll soon be getting dark and we can sleep under that fallen beech tree. We might even be able to cat-ch a wood mouse or two for supper.'

They awoke as the sun rose, stretched their legs, and wandered along the footpath through the wood towards the cottage. A squirrel scampered up an oak tree. The wood was carpeted with the whites of wood anemones and greater stitchwort, clumps of primroses, and the deeper yellows of lesser celandine. A few bluebells had begun to appear but the trees had yet to burst into leaf.

They emerged from the wood and followed a pawpath that ran alongside a field. A skylark fluttered high in the sky above them singing a lonely song. Jet stopped and lifted her nose towards the sky.

'Can you sniff what I'm sniffing?' she asked Clem. They looked behind to see a cat following them in the distance.

'Yer alroight, me litt-ul darlings?' miaowed the cat when it caught up with them. 'Ow yer gettin' on?' Yer 'edding zouth to the zea are yuh? Cos, if zo, yer 'edding in the wrong direction.'

They turned to see a black and white tom. Jet recognised him immediately.

'It's my old friend Do-it-tomorrow Tommo!' she exclaimed rubbing his nose warmly with her nose. 'We met long ago at the catmint in Clawdia's garden. You said you'd return the following day for another nip, but you didn't show up.'

'Oi 'ad other business in 'em days,' replied Tommo proudly.

Jet explained that they were going to the intercounty strays' office to get a collar for Clem and re-activate her own.

'Yerl need 'em collars in this land,' said Tommo, 'Cats around 'ere bee ever zo precious about their territory. Oi don't 'av a collar mezelf cos every cat tween 'ere and the Zolent knows me. Oi bee up from 'Amble mezelf.'

'Where's 'Amble?' asked Clem.

'Tiz in 'Ampshire near to the Zolent. Oi can take thee there, but not today. Oi bee back tomorrow though.

Oi bee off 'ome then cos the natives moight bee gettin' restless. Yuh can come with me if you loik.'

Jet politely declined his offer. The three cats continued to walk along the pawpath chatting amicably. When they reached another copse the path petered out with not a pawprint in sight.

'Go past that old chalk pit and keep on goin' through the trees until yuh pick up the scent of a public pawpath,' said Tommo. 'Trek along there until yer zee a purr-missive path that belongs to 'umans. That leads to a lane. There yerl zee a soign to Slowdown. Follow it and turn to the roight. Av-ter 'arf a mile yerl zee the cottage on the left. Nice taaking to yuh. Oi bee off now.'

Jet and Clem soon found the cottage. They could easily have missed it. It was a dilapidated old dwelling hidden behind a high and ragged hawthorn hedge. They entered through a partially open gate and a gap in a rotten door into a hallway that led to a musty room clouded with cobwebs.

A scrawny old cat with dry grey eyes and white whiskers confronted them. He moved unsteadily to a creaky coffee table in the corner of the room near a window that looked out on to a garden full of overgrown shrubs. He sat down slowly behind the table.

'Will ticket number one go to desk number one,' he croaked.

There were no other cats in the room apart from Clem and Jet. Clem could not see any tickets.

'Go and stand opposite him,' said Jet. 'He's the only bureau-cat here, but he likes to make out he's important. His nick-name is "Purr-fectly Obvious". It's his cat-ch phrase – you'll see.'

'Just the ticket!' said the bureau-cat wearily when Clem approached the table. Clem showed him his empty paws and muttered that he did not have a ticket.

'What now?' he asked.

'It's purr-fectly obvious,' said the bureau-cat. 'Fill it in.'

He slammed a piece of pay-purr onto the desk.

Clem looked bewildered.

'It's an appli-cat-ion form for an intercounty stray purr-mit. You must write down answers to all the questions,' mumbled the bureau-cat.

Jet joined Clem at the desk and murmured in his ear *sotto voce*: 'Show him your oil-stained paw and pretend it's painful – put it close to his eyes so he can see it.'

The bureau-cat stared at the paw and then at Clem and Jet.

'My friend injured his writing paw in a farmyard – so he can't write at the moment,' said Jet.

Clem screwed up his eyes and winced as if in pain.

'What should he do now?' asked Jet.

'It's purr-fectly obvious' said the bureau-cat. 'You must read the questions to him and scratch down his answers on the pay-purr.'

Jet started reading. There were two sides to fill in.

'Question one: what's your name?' asked Jet.

'Clem,' said Clem proudly.

Jet wrote it down.

'Question two: What are you?'

'A stray.'

'Smoking is not purr-mitted,' said the old bureau-cat severely.

Clem was puzzled. Jet whispered in his ear. 'He's hard of hearing and thinks you said "ashtray". I'll write down "a stray" below your name.'

'Question three: are you a lost stray?'

Clem wasn't sure if he was lost or not because he was with Jet, and she knew where they were. Jet told him to say 'yes.'

'Question four: Where were you lost?' asked Jet loudly and then, adding quietly: 'Anything will do, Clem. Purr-fectly Obvious won't look at the answers I write down – he just wants your money.'

'Up in 'Ampshire,' said Clem with the hint of a smile.

Jet wrote down: 'Amble'.

'Now we get to the claws,' said the bureau-cat turning over the pay-purr and slamming it back on the desk.

'What do you mean?' asked Clem alarmed.

'It's purr-fectly obvious,' said Purr-fectly Obvious. 'Terms and conditions apply. Read and confirm that you have read them and agree to claws one, claws two, claws three, and claws four.'

Jet read them out aloud: 'Claws one: A stray, hitherto known as the appli-cat, should not enter another cat's territory without purr-mission – except in the absence of the aforesaid territory owner and/or one or more of her or his representatives.

'Claws two: An appli-cat, when confronted by the aforesaid territory owner and/or one or more of her or his representatives, should stop, sit down, look at the aforesaid territory owner and/or one or more of her or his representatives submissively and admiringly, lift her or his head to reveal the intercounty stray collar, and purr for at least two minutes. The appli-cat thereby seeks official purr-mission to enter the territory according to the rules and regulations of current stray cat legislation. If this does not secure the purr-mission of the aforesaid territory owner and/or one or more of her or his representatives, the appli-cat should roll over on her or his back and wave her or his paws in the air.

'Claws three: the applicat should, wherever possible, position her or his body and head upwind or upbreeze from the aforesaid territory owner and/or one or more of her or his representatives to enable the intercounty stray collar scent to waft freely and without help or hindrance towards the aforesaid territory owner and/or one or more of her or his representatives.

'Claws four: when confronted by the aforesaid territory owner and/or one or more of her or his representatives, the appli-cat should never hiss, bare her or his teeth, arch her or his back, or wag her or his tail angrily.'

The bureau-cat put a paw to his mouth and yawned. 'Now sign the pay-purr,' he said forgetting that Jet had told him Clem had injured his paw and could not write.

Jet pointed to the bottom of the page and whispered to Clem: 'Scratch a cross here and I'll sign as a witness below.'

She removed her collar and pushed it across the desk to the bureau-cat. 'I would be most grateful if you would also be good enough to reactivate my collar,' she said in her polite voice. 'It is scented out.'

'That will be two and tuppence ape-knee reduced from half-a-crown for two stray collars,' said the bureau-cat. 'That's two bob for the stray registration fee and collar activation, and tuppence ape-knee reduced from sixpence for the collar reactivation.'

'But I don't have any money,' said Clem.

Jet padded some pebbles and old bits of pay-purr across the desk. The bureau-cat seemed satisfied and brushed them into a drawer in his desk.

'Clem, you are now a registered intercounty stray,' said the old cat with a condescending smile. 'Congratulations. You are now officially a stray. You may wander without fear or flavour, I mean favour, throughout the feline world.'

He turned his back on Clem and Jet and disappeared into an adjoining room in the cottage. After some ten minutes he re-appeared carrying two pale blue collars, a piece of cotton wool, and a bottle containing an oily brown liquid. He poured some of the thick liquid onto the cotton wool, sniffed it, nodded with approval, and dabbed the liquid onto each collar.

'Made up fresh this morning, ready for immediate appli-cat-ion,' he said. 'My own blend. It is most consistent and purr-sistent and should keep you both going for at least a couple of months, or longer if the weather gets cold again. Wear the collars all the time and guard them with your nine lives.'

Jet fastened the collar around Clem's neck and put on her own. They thanked the bureau-cat and bid him farewell.

'Now, before we proceed further on our search for Catrina, I think it's time you had a little schooling,' said Jet.

Chapter Five

A LITTLE SCHOOLING

'This is open territory,' said Jet. 'It is not registered. We are free to stay or stray.' The two cats had wandered from the cottage for a couple of miles along the lane and turned left into a wood on the edge of another field.

Clem sat down and purred. He was feeling happier now he had a collar with a scent purr-mit.

'How can you tell it's open territory?' asked Clem.

'Easy,' replied Jet as she sat down. 'I haven't had a sniff of a cat for the past hour.'

After their rest, they stood up, looked ahead, and froze. They could see a bright yellow animal on the other side of the field creeping towards them.

'What is it?' asked Clem.

'I don't know,' replied Jet.

As it got nearer, they realised it was a haggard brown cat wearing a yellow visibility jacket.

'Are you sure we've have purr-mission to be here?' mumbled Clem touching his collar to make sure it was still there.

'Keep calm,' replied Jet. She noticed the cat was wearing a red and white collar with the letters MRC on it.

'Good-day to you both,' said the brown cat stopping in front of them.

'Are you looking for the Intercounty Strays' Office?' asked Jet.

'Oh no! I have my own collar,' said the brown cat pointing to her collar.

Jet had never seen a collar like it.

'What does MRC mean?' she asked.

'I'm a mountain rescue cat.'

Jet and Clem look at each other in amazement.

'But there are no mountains in Hampshire or Sussex, just hills and chalk downs,' said Jet.

'Yes, I know. It's an easy job,' replied the brown cat with a twinkle in her eye that indi-cat-ed she was joking.

'I'm curious: what do you really do?'

'I'm not working in this county or even looking for work. I'm here because I got carried away. I'm not a stray. I'm going home.'

The brown cat said she lived in the Lake District near some mountains and hills that humans call fells.

'Some are named after us. Have you heard of Cat-stye Cam or Blen-cat-hra?'

The two strays shook their heads.

'You must have heard of Cat Bells?'

'Oh yes,' said Clem missing the point completely. 'I've met pet cats that wear collars with bells to scare away birds and mice and let humans know where they are in case they get lost.'

The brown cat smiled. 'Cat Bells is a fell in the Lake District.'

'You said you got carried away,' said Jet. 'Is that why you are here and not there?'

The brown cat explained that a few days ago, she was by herself getting ready for work when she noticed a family picnicking. She managed to jump into the boot of their car without them noticing and help herself to some delicious line-caught salmon. The family returned before she could finish the meal, so she squeezed under a blanket to hide.

'It was a long journey. When the car stopped, the family opened the boot and I escaped. So here I am. I'm going back up north to my owners. They will wonder where I am. They've probably sent out search parties looking for me and posted missing cat notices all over the Lake District fells with my picture on it.'

'Have you seen a calico around here?' asked Clem opportunistically and, now that he had learnt the meaning of the word, a little proudly. 'She has a black, orange, and white coat and bright blue eyes. She was heading south to the sea. Her name is Catrina.'

'Catrina? I don't think I've seen her,' said the mountain rescue cat. 'But I did pass an old Siamese tom sitting outside a hut hidden in the bushes near Lowadown Lake about a mile south of here. He was white and wearing a black cap and gown. He might be able to help you.'

'That's where we're going,' said Jet. 'It's a school.'

'Is that on our route south to the sea?' asked Clem after saying goodbye to the brown cat. He had already forgotten that she had suggested he needed some schooling.

'If you are to find Catrina, you will need to learn a few things – like reading and writing,' replied Jet. 'How else will you be able to read the signposts or renew your intercounty stray purr-mit when the scent has completely evaporated.'

'But you will be with me.'

'We could get separated,' said Jet ominously. 'You never know.'

The two strays followed a shallow chalk stream teaming with trout. Swans and ducks drifted lazily in the water. They soon found Lowadown Lake but could not see the hut. The pawpath around the lake had become overrun by bushes, brambles, and nettles.

'The hut is a long-forgotten bird hide that humans used to use to spy on birds,' explained Jet. 'I remember coming here a few years ago when I was young.'

The two hapless cats searched around for the path in the undergrowth. Jet stopped beneath a fuchsia bush at the side of the stream and stared straight ahead.

'This is the school,' she said when the hut came into view. 'Clawdia told me last month that it has a teacher but hasn't had any pupils for months.'

They crawled out of the bush and leapt over the stream.

A sign above the school entrance read: 'EduCATion, EduCATion, EduCATion' in large black letters'.

The ageing Siamese with the black cap and gown emerged from the hide to greet them. 'My name is Purr C. Veer,' he said with a friendly voice. 'I am the head teacher here and you are most welcome.'

Jet explained that her friend Clem required some schooling to help him look for his sister Catrina.

'You've come to the right place,' replied Purr C. Veer joyfully. He pointed to a display board inside the entrance of the hut. It read: 'This school is renowned for its dediCATion to eduCATion. We are able to inculCATe lots of lovely learning into any CAT.'

He pulled a dusty sheet of paper from under a table and pawed it to Clem.

'The silly puss for the entrance exam!' he said smiling warmly.

Clem frowned and cast a glance at Jet. She examined the page and read the first word.

'It says syllabus,' she said, grinning.

'Before we accept you, you must pass the entrance exam,' said the head teacher. 'Say after me: "Mice are nice on ice if you splice with rice and a slice of spice. Lice will not suffice".'

'Mice are nice on rice if you splice with spice and a slice of lice. Ice will not suffice,' said Clem.

'Excellent!' said the head teacher removing his cap and bowing. 'You have passed the entrance test and are now enrolled on the course.'

He pawed a torn piece of paper to Clem.

'Please read it.' said Purr C. Veer.

'I can't read,' replied Clem.

'Excellent! Then I will recite it from memory and I want you to repeat it: Smile at us, pay us, pass us; but do not quite forget; For we are the cats of England, that never have spoken yet.'

Clem repeated it as best he could.

'Excellent! Now repeat: Yes, I remember Adlestrop, and willows, willow-herb, and grass, and meadowsweet, and haycocks dry, and cat-kins many. And for that minute a cat purred.'

Clem cleared his throat and repeated it although he was not sure if he had remembered all the words.

'Excellent!' said the head teacher, snatching the paper from Clem's paw and pawing him another piece of pay-purr containing a list of words. 'That was your first lesson. You now have a minute to look through the courses we offer and choose your second lesson.'

'But I've just told him I can't read,' Clem mumbled to himself. He felt uncomfortable at being put under pressure. He turned to Jet for help.

'Pretend to look,' she said.

'Well?' asked Purr C. Veer after a minute had elapsed. 'What have you chosen?'

'Languages,' replied Clem, guessing that they were included in the list.

'Excellent,' said Purr C. Veer. 'What language?'

'French.'

'We don't teach French.'

'German, then.'

'We don't teach German.'

'Can I learn Latin?'

'We don't teach Latin.'

'What languages do you teach?'

'Good question. Cat-alan.'

'Cat-alan?'

'Only Cat-alan.'

Jet shook her head at Clem.

'I don't want to learn Cat-alan,' said Clem.

'Choose another topic,' said the master.

Clem looked at the list and guessed again.

'History.'

'Excellent subject. I'm sure you know all about Louis Cat Oars and the kings of France. Our own history originated in Purr-shah, but unfortunately our only Purr-shun teacher left last year. So, history is off the curriculum at the moment.'

'How about geography?'

'Excellent choice. We can teach you all about Cat-ford, Cat-terick, and Cat-alonia.'

Jet shook her head again.

'Zoology?' asked Clem.

'Ah! Cat-fish and cat-erpillars,' said the master. 'Some of our lower brethren. My favourites. But we don't have any here. They all died in the winter.'

'Do you teach domestic science?'

'An excellent topic. Learning to cat-er for cats. But we are a bit short of food. If you come back next week, we might be able to oblige.'

'All I want to do is learn to read and write,' said Clem boldly.

'Excellent. So why not stay here until you can?'

'Excellent!' repeated Clem reassured that he would not have to learn about Cat-ford and cat-erpillars.

He turned to Jet for approval. But she had disappeared.

Chapter Six

THE KINGFISHER

Clem looked for Jet along the stream, around Lowadown Lake, and in the hedgerows, but there was not a sight, sign, sound, or smell of her. He guessed she must have found a way through the reeds and greater pond sedge to the shore of the lake.

'Do you think she paddled through the water where it is shallow looking for fish to eat?' he asked Purr C. Veer when he arrived back at the bird hide. 'Surely, she wouldn't have left without saying goodbye.'

The head teacher listened attentively and proved most sympathetic. 'I'm sure she left with the best of intentions,' he said. 'In my view, you would do no better than stay here and learn to read and write. It would help in your search not only for your sister but also for Jet.'

Clem put a paw to his whiskers and thought for a moment. 'Yes, I think that would be good idea,' he said finally.

'You are the first pupil I've had for months, so I can offer you one-to-one tuition,' said Purr C. Veer enthusiastically. 'I do not expect a fee but I would be most grateful if you could bring me back the occasional fish, field mouse, water vole, or sparrow when you go out. My legs are now getting weary so I cannot get about as well as I used to. I will be happy with whatever you bring back.'

Clem agreed to go hunting for him but pointed out that if Jet did not return, he would have to leave as soon as he had learnt to read and write.

'Of course,' said the head teacher, using his gown to wipe a drop of spittle from his mouth. 'Finding Jet and Catrina must be your top priority.'

The lessons were intense and Clem made rapid progress. He soon learnt to write his name and simple messages in his own paw-writing. Every lunchtime he headed out of the hide to look for lunch and find a meal for Purr C. Veer.

One day, he was crouching on the shore of the lake munching his lunch when he saw a bright blue flash. The next minute, he heard a voice.

'Do you know what the K problem is?'

Clem looked up and to his surprise saw a kingfisher purr-ched above him on a branch of an oak tree.

'No, I don't know,' replied Clem.

'Ha! Ha! Very funny, but very good,' said the kingfisher. 'Old PCV is a great teacher and he's obviously teaching you well. He's a good friend of mine. Did he ask you to find him lunch?'

'Yes.'

'He always knows a cat with a good nose for hunting.'

'Really?'

'I used to listen to his lessons. That's how I learnt the Queen's English. I'm now the king of the kingfishers around here. My name is Kingsley.'

Clem introduced himself and then continued eating.

'That's a nice knife you have there,' said Kingsley.

'I don't have a knife.'

'That's the K problem. Do you want to hear my K song?'

'I'll listen while I finish my lunch,' muttered Clem.

'The knight rode through the night,' sang the kingfisher. 'There was not a knot in his reins. While his lady napped in the knapweed, the rains came, "The kingfisher reigns." shouted the knight. What do you think? I made it up.'

'Excellent!' said Clem wryly in a voice mimicking the head teacher. 'Have you seen a tricoloured cat with blue eyes on one of your flights? Her name is Catrina. She's my sister. She was heading south to the sea.'

'Catrina? I don't think I've seen her.'

'Have you seen a black stray with green eyes on your travels?'

'How many lost sisters do you have?'

'The black cat is my friend and a stray like me,' said Clem pointing to his blue collar. 'Her name is Jet.'

'Yes, I have seen her. She was heading north to the great unknown.'

'Great unknown?'

'I'm the post-bird around her, but I can only go so far before I fly into enemy territory.'

'Post-bird?'

'I collect and deliver messages, just like the messenger pigeons in the Great War. Can you climb trees?'

'Yes.'

'Good. You look like a grown cat who doesn't groan, so let's do a deal. While I'm away on message duty, would you like to defend my territory around the lake and along the stream until I come back. It should only take an hour or so during your lunch break. If you see another kingfisher on one of my purr-ches, all you have to do is dart up the tree and shout "s-cat-ter". That will frighten it away. Agreed?'

'No!' said Clem angrily. 'There's nothing in it for me.'

'I'll bring you minnows and sticklebacks galore – enough for you and poor old PCV.'

'Agreed!'

The kingfisher flew off towards the stream and after a couple of minutes returned with a minnow in his beak. He dropped it at Clem's paws and quickly returned with another before flying off over the lake. Clem finished his lunch and wandered back to the hut with the two minnows in his mouth.

He recounted the meeting to the head teacher.

'Oh, I know that blue bird,' he said. 'Kingsley was always hovering and fluttering around here when I used to give lessons. What you agreed to do is a classic example of a symbiotic relationship.'

'Symbiotic? What does that mean?' asked Clem.

'The bird gives something to you and you give something back,' explained the head teacher. 'It's mutually beneficial. It's a bit like tit for tat.'

'I did see a long-tailed tit when I come to think about it but I didn't cat-ch it or give it to him,' said Clem somewhat bewildered. 'I don't think I saw any tats. In fact, I don't know what they are.'

The following lunch time, Clem set out to meet Kingsley again and ask him about tits and tats. He sat hungrily beneath the oak tree watching for enemy kingfishers and waiting for his lunch to arrive. On seeing the blue flash of a kingfisher, he scrambled up the tree to the lowest branch and prepared to shout 's-cat-ter.' But he wasn't sure if the bird was friend or foe.

'It's only me,' said Kingsley purr-ching on a branch above him. 'If you jump down, I'll fetch you a stickleback.'

His friend returned within a minute and thumped the wriggling fish against a branch to kill it. He dropped it down to Clem.

'I'll sing you my R song while you eat,' said Kingsley. 'The kingfisher seized the reins as the rains came. That's why the kingfisher reigns supreme.'

'That's part of your K song,' said Clem, looking up from his lunch. 'You sang that yesterday,'

The bird flew away and returned with another fish for Clem to take to Purr C. Veer.

'I refuse to empty the refuse bin,' he sang. 'Because I've just read a book you can't read. And now I want to record a record of my song: 'I poured my whole supply of water into a bucket with a hole in it. A whole hole – ho! Ho!'

Clem interrupted. 'Do you know what tats are?' he said sheepishly.

Kingsley did not know. 'Do you mean kit for cat?'

The stray and kingfisher continued to meet every lunch-time. The days lengthened and the flowers in the hedgerows blossomed. Clem soon became familiar with the land around the lake and stream. He prided himself on his ex-purr-tise in scaring off any bird that dared to encroach on his friend's territory.

'I've heard on the bird-vine that there's a message for you,' said Kingsley one day. The following lunch time, the kingfisher was waiting for Clem in the tree with a piece of paper in his beak. He allowed it to flutter down in the breeze to the ground near two dead minnows that he had already caught. It was a message from Jet. It said simply: 'C. Can you read and write now? Best, J.' Clem pawed 'yes' on the paper, climbed up the tree and passed it to his friend.

'I'll be away for several days,' said Kingsley. 'Guard my territory with your nine lives. You'll find plenty of juicy water voles for lunch on the banks of the stream.'

Clem waited over lunch for several days but the bird did not appear. He was beginning to fear the worst. Maybe the bird had been killed by a buzzard or a farmer with a shotgun. And then, just as he was giving up hope, he saw the blue flash of his friend. He had a message in his beak. It read: 'C. Meet me at the cat-hedral. Best, J.'

Chapter Seven

CALL TO PRAYER

Clem and Purr C. Veer sat outside the school finishing their supper and staring up in awe at the night sky.

'That's the Milky Way,' observed the head teacher. 'There are hundreds of billions of stars out there. They are billions and billions of miles away.'

Clem blinked and hesitated. 'I'm leaving,' he blurted out. 'It's a good starlit night to leave.'

Purr C. Veer turned to him in surprise.

'Now you've learnt to read and write, you've finally decided to resume your search for Jet and Catrina. Is that your purr-puss?'

'Jet sent me a message,' said Clem. 'She told me to go straight to the cat-hedral. Do you know where that is?'

'I used to go there when I was young and fit,' he replied. 'It's not difficult to find. Go around the shore to the other side of the lake. You should then head south into an ancient woodland and cross two large fields. If you walk briskly, you will arrive by sunrise. Continue south along a pawpath through another wood. Watch out for the yellow archangel.'

Clem looked up at him. 'Yellow archangel? Will she take me to the cat-hedral?'

'It's a yellow wild flower that grows in woods at this time of the year,' replied the head teacher kindly. 'When you come out of the wood, you will reach a meadow. On the other side you will see the cathedral in the centre of the remnants of an abandoned village. There is also a monastery in a hamlet known as Goindown about a mile from the village.'

'What's the name of the village?'

'Nilldown. It's well known to locals. Look out for a public pawpath known as the Via Duomo. Someone is sure to come out and greet you. They are friendly there. And don't forget the most important lesson I taught you, an edu-cat-ed cat is always be able to …'

'Entertain a new idea, entertain a friend, and entertain itself.'

'Excellent! Now off you go and travel safely. My regards to Jet when you see her.'

Clem thanked Purr C. Veer, said goodbye, wandered to the other side of the lake, followed a scent trail south through the woods, and trudged slowly across the first field as directed by Purr C. Veer. 'I'm not as fit as I used to be,' he murmured to himself. Feeling tired after the trek, he hid under some branches in a ditch on the far side of the field and fell fast asleep.

The next day, before the sun rose, he was woken up by the faintest of miaows coming from the ancient woodland. He could not make out the cat in the darkness of the early morning and he could not smell any scent. A breeze was blowing north towards the other cat.

Clem thought the cat might possibly be the territory chief. He decided to play safe and heed claws two of the intercounty stray regulations. He sat down submissively and purred loudly as the cat approached across the field.

'No need to roll over!' shouted the cat.

Clem immediately recognised Jet's voice. She had been following in his smelly paw-steps some distance behind and was planning to cat-ch up with him by the time he reached the cat-hedral.

'Why did you leave me at the school?' he asked.

'If you are to be successful in your search for Catrina, you need to learn not only to read and write but also to stand on your own four paws. In any case, I went back to see Clawdia. She keeps abreast of all the mews and is even more familiar with Hampshire and Sussex than me.'

'What did she say?'

'She said that because of inclement weather conditions a few weeks ago, all scent of Catrina had been blown and washed away. According to all her garden friends, there had not been a sniff of Catrina between Uppandown and Lowadown since then. Our only hope, she said, now that we're having a fine spell of weather, was to try to pick up her scent south of Lowadown. I then bid her goodbye and hastened back to the school. Purr C. Veer told me you had just left.'

'Have you been to the cat-hedral before?' asked Clem.

'Oh yes!' replied Jet. 'I know these woods only too well. I was born near Nilldown and wandered around this area for days after escaping from the drowning in the bucket.'

They crossed another field and followed a well-trodden pawpath through a copse.

'Yellow archangel,' said Clem proudly pointing to a sprinkling of the flowers in the wood. He wanted her to know that his schooling had not been in vain.

'One of my favourite flowers,' said Jet smugly. 'You find lots of them growing in the Slithadown and Uppandown woods during the spring and summer.'

The two strays came to a glade. Clem pointed to a spot in front of his paws. A passing cat had scratched an arrow and two words in the ground.

'What does it say?' asked Jet.

'Via Duomo,' replied Clem.

Jet was impressed that Clem could now read. They continued along the track, crossed the meadow that Purr C. Veer had mentioned, and came to a village full of crumbling buildings with broken windows and unhinged doors.

'Nilldown was abandoned when the soldiers took it over as a range to practice firing their weapons,' explained Jet. 'It's not far from the cottage where Ma-Puss gave birth to Clawdia and me.'

The two strays wandered along a street to the centre of the village where they spotted a stagnant pond and a derelict church. A tall upright black cat immediately emerged through a gap in a side entrance to the church. Clem and Jet sank to their knees, in accordance with the intercounty stray regulations, hummed friendly purrs, and gazed admiringly at him. They noticed that he was wearing a white collar around his neck.

'Do not be afraid,' said the cat stretching out a paw. 'My name is Father Felix. Are you pilgrims?'

Jet and Clem introduced themselves. 'We are strays,' explained Jet.

'How wonderful to meet you,' replied Father Felix. 'Welcome to St Cat-herine's Cat-hedral. We welcome all waifs, walkers, wanderers, wayfarers, strays, vagabonds, vagrants, travellers, tramps, beggars, minstrels, mendicants, itinerants, pilgrims, ramblers, refugees, sundowners, the homeless, the sick, the infirm, the injured, and the faithful to our beautiful cat-hedral.'

The two strays stared at the white collar. They had not seen that type of collar before.

'It's a clerical collar worn by the clergy in churches of various denominations,' said Father Felix.

Jet and Clem seemed confused by the explanation.

'Some people call it a dog collar,' he said.

Jet and Clem arched their backs in fright and almost jumped out of their skins thinking he might be a dog dressed up as a cat.

'Fear not, I shall not attack you or bark impre-cat-ions at you,' said Father Felix. 'I'm not a wolf in sheep's clothing. I'm a cat-holic priest. Would you like to see around our cat-hedral and purr-haps paws for a moment of reflection?'

Clem was not sure.

'Paws for thought?' he said turning to Jet.

'Paws to pray for a successful outcome to our search for Catrina,' she replied.

'I shall pray that your prayers for Catrina will be answered,' said the priest-cat. 'Let me assure you that we are not dog-matic in our humble place of worship. We avoid pontifi-cat-ion at all costs. Would you like to visit our lovely cat-holic school.'

He led them through a wooden door and along a passage to a large dusty room full of little cats squatting on their haunches listening to a slim young female cat. She was wearing a black headdress.

'Some of the kittens here are as poor as church mice, excuse the expression,' said Father Felix. 'We have a team of volunteers who read to them, pray with them, and bring in food, milk, pens, and pencils. May I introduce you to Sister Pawline who is our youth leader. She has a great sense of humour which the pupils love.'

Father Felix explained quietly that Sister Pawline had taken a vow of poverty and lived alone in a small cell furnished with just an old prayer mat.

'Eyes closed and paws together,' she told the class. 'Now recite the magnifi-cat in silence to yourselves while I welcome our guests.'

Sister Pawline wandered across to greet Jet and Clem. 'Welcome,' she said with a warm smile. 'Are you roaming Cat-holics?'

'They are strays from afar,' interposed the priest-cat. 'They'd love to hear one of your class recite the magnifi-cat.'

Sister Pawline turned to the class and clapped her paws. They opened their eyes, sprang to attention, and gathered around Father Felix and the two guests.

'Who can recite the magnifi-cat?' she asked. Every kitten raised an enthusiastic paw. Sister Pawline beckoned to a kitten at the back, saying: 'He hath put down the mighty cats from their seat: and hath exalted the humble and meek. Now continue!'

'He hath filled the hungry cats with good things: and the rich he hath sent empty away,' said the kitten.

'Well done Kitty,' said Sister Pawline. 'Now all of you go back to your places and write in your best paw-writing: 'the cat next to the hat begat a kitten on a mat.'

Clem whispered to Jet. 'Purr C. Veer would be most impressed.'

'In the next lesson, the kittens will be taught the cat-echism,' said Father Felix. 'But we won't wait for that.'

Jet and Clem followed him along the corridor into a small darkened room with several small cushions and, in the middle of the room, what appeared to be a wooden box on top of another wooden box. 'Let's stop here for a minute and pray quietly,' said the priest-cat. 'Cats that stray together often like to pray together when they come here.'

The two strays kneeled next to Father Felix and whispered a silent prayer for the success of their search for Catrina. Clem wondered how all this prayer and silence might help him to find his sister. He felt a sudden spasm of sadness and two tears seeped from his eyes.

The priest-cat and Jet did not notice and concentrated on their prayers. Jet opened her eyes and allowed them to adjust to the gloom of the darkened room. 'What's that?' she asked pointing to the two wooden boxes.

'The top box is a coffin,' replied the priest. 'It contains the body of one of our most famous cats, may she rest in peace. The lower box is a cat-afalque.'

Jet and Clem squinted to read the inscription on the cat-afalque: 'Pussy cat, pussy cat, where have you been? I've been to London to visit the Queen.'

'Why have you left the coffin here?' enquired Jet.

'So we can pay our respects,' explained Father Felix. "Ten strong cats of noble birth and good upbringing will then take the coffin and cat-afalque to the cat-hedral cat-acombs. They will put the coffin next to the coffins of two of our other famous cats: the cat that played the fiddle when the cow jumped over the moon and the cat that went to sea with an owl in a beautiful pea-green boat. The three cats are all in purr-gatory undergoing purr-ifi-cat-ion. They will wait there until St Peter calls them to ascend into heaven through the purr-ley gates. There are twelve gates, you know.'

Jet and Clem took their leave of Father Felix and made their way out respectfully through the cat-hedral's cloisters.

'Do you now feel sufficiently uplifted to continue our search for Catrina?' Jet asked Clem.

'I'm beginning to feel sad again,' responded Clem with a grimace. 'I don't know where we'll go now. My prayers haven't been answered.'

He looked up to heaven and noticed a blue bird with an orange chest purr-ched in a tree above the village pond. He immediately recognised Kingsley the kingfisher.

The bird flew out of the tree, dropped a piece of notepaper to the ground, and flew away without so much as a chirp.

Jet picked the paper up and read the message aloud: 'Dear Clem, I hope what I write is right, because I can't see the white in the Isle of Wight. Clawdia has just received a report, as yet unconfirmed. There has been a sight of Catrina at a site near the History of the Cat Mewseum in the Goindown monastery. She heard it on the cat-vine. No more mews. I hope you find her soon. Good luck. K the k.'

Chapter Eight

THE HISTORY OF THE CAT

The two hapless strays discovered the History of the Cat Mewseum in the ruins of the monastery. They stopped outside to read warnings displayed at the entrance:

Visitors may find some of the sights, sounds, and scenes in the mewseum upsetting. Some exhibits have flashing images.

BEWARE! Curiosity killed the cat.

'Let's look around the exhibits and see if we can see or smell Catrina,' said Jet. 'Can you remember her smell?'

'I'll never forget it,' replied Clem.

They found their way to an introductory exhibit where a brown tabby and a grey cat were arguing in front of a poster.

'A molecule is superior to an atom,' said the tabby. 'I should know, because my name is Molly Cool.'

'No, you are wrong,' said the grey. 'An atom is definitely inferior to a molecule. I should know because I'm a tom and my name is Atom.'

'So you agree,' said the tabby. 'A molecule must have at least two atoms. It must be superior.'

The grey thought for a moment. 'Let's take a vote on it.'

'But there only two of us, how can we?'

'One of us could abstain.'

The two squabbling cats moved away allowing the two strays to study the display. It read:

In the beginning was the atom, and the atom was with the molecule. The atoms and molecules became dinosaurs. After the dinosaurs came the cats. They were brilliant. They invented everything – agriculture, religion, medicine, science – and provided the glue for the English language. This mewseum tells the story of the cat, how cats suffered when humanity took over, and the ongoing legacy of cats going forward.

'We all know that cats are the cleverest animals on earth,' pawed the celebrated wordsmith T. S. Cleverpuss in her classic wartime memoir: Old Cats Never Die. (Catsgood Press, 1919). 'We have always kept it a secret, though. We let humans think they are much more intelligent. But they learnt almost everything from us.'

Jet and Clem agreed that this was most interesting but just a little challenging and confusing. Catrina was nowhere to be seen.

The two strays followed the squabbling cats to another poster. Jet turned to Clem and pointed a paw at the words. He took the hint and read aloud the title of the poster: 'How cats named life on Earth.'

They studied the photos on the poster intently. 'Catkins, caterpillars, octopus – that was a crafty one, kittiwake,' said Clem.

Their lips drooled when they saw pictures of catnip. 'If only we could get some of that now,' sighed Jet.

Another poster showed pictures of famous human heroines named after cats: Cat-herine of Aragon, Cat-herine the Great, Cat-herine of Siena. 'They are all ancient Cat-heroines,' said Jet who liked to boast that she was familiar with cat history. 'They have silent 'o's. Humans like to drop the 'o's in their spellings. Can you think of any modern human cat-heroines that are famous?'

Clem thought for a while and tried to remember the radio and TV programmes he had heard before the flood swept everything away from his home. 'Catherine, Duchess of Cambridge,' he said proudly. 'Cat-herine Zeta-Jones and Cat-herine Deneuve.'

'Exactly, there have been lots of human cat-heroines with silent 'o's throughout our history. And lots of singers. Think of Cat Stevens and Kitty Wells.'

Clem mew-sed for a moment. The name Kitty Wells brought to mind an old nursery rhyme. He began to sing: 'Ding, dong, bell, Pussy's in the well. Who put her in? Kitty in the kitchen.'

'That reminds me, we forgot Cat-herine Cookson,' replied Jet. 'But this is all very a-mew-sing. We're getting carried away, so let's move on.'

The third exhibit extolled the impact of cats on discovering various types of illness and medical conditions. There were several displays.

'What's that?' asked Clem pointing a paw at wax models of two black and white cats with large eyes inside a glass display. The lenses of the eyes of one of the cats were noticeably cloudy. The other cat had sparking green eyes and was crouching in the centre of a road. A series of metal domes containing reflective glass spheres ran along the centre of the road

'The cat on the left has cat-aracts, or more specifically feline cat-aracts,' explained Jet. 'We invented the metal domes to improve road safety for humans. They are known as cat's eyes. They reflect the headlights of cars when it's dark.'

The next display showed a cat lying on its back with all four legs raised in the air beside a cardboard cut-out of a Welsh dragon. The sign below the model said. 'Mew-rig has cat-alepsy.' Another cat appeared frozen on all four legs. 'Catty from Cat-terick is cat-atonic' read the caption.

'Uh! I wouldn't like to have cat-aracts, or cat-alepsy, or be cat-atonic,' said Clem.

As they moved to the next exhibit, they heard bleating and the sound of a mews-ical instrument.

'Is that cat-erwauling?' he asked.

'No, it sounds like sheep baa-ing and human mew-sic' replied Jet.

They entered a door with 'Adults only' emblazoned on it. A video clip played three scenes repeatedly. In the first, several sheep in a field looked towards a camera and bleated. The second showed a human preparing cords from the intestines of a sheep. The final scene had a young woman playing a violin while a man and a woman played tennis.

'It's all about cat-gut,' said Jet. 'It's used to make the strings for mews-ical instruments and tennis rackets.'

'Shouldn't it be called sheep-gut?' asked Clem

'Trust humans to get that wrong.'

The next exhibit was called 'Cat-astrophe.' Scores of cats cowered before a sailor who was whipping an emaciated tabby cat tied to the rigging of the ship.

'The cats on board the ship have mew-tinied because of poor living conditions and little food,' commented Jet. 'That poor cat is being made an example of. The cat has been keelhauled I think. If you look closely you see that he – or it could be a she - is a soggy moggy. The sailor is now flogging it with a cat o'nine tails. The captain complains that they promised to keep to their daily rat cat-ch quota but haven't. He says they are purr-fidious.'

Clem turned away. By now, he was feeling a little nauseous and getting bored with the exhibits. He pointedly walked past another exhibit entitled 'Cat-aclysm.' It showed cats swimming for their lives in a flooded river.

Jet realised it reminded him of the flood that led to Catrina's disappearance.

'I need some fresh air,' moaned Clem. He desperately wanted to resume his search for Catrina.

Outside the mewseum, they found Molly Cool and Atom having a smoke under a yew tree. The two were now cat-chatting away in a most friendly way.

'We are looking for my sister Catrina,' said Clem. 'Have you seen her? We had a report of a sighting near here. She is tricoloured with sparkling blue eyes.'

'She was here yesterday,' said Molly Cool casually.

'You missed her,' added Atom.

Clem did not find their replies helpful.

'Which way did she go?' he asked anxiously.

The two smokers explained that she went south towards the convention.

'It's an annual event, but we're not going this year,' said Molly Cool. 'We have to get back to the laboratories where we work.'

'How do we find this convention?' asked Clem.

'You see that down over there with cat-tle moving up it?'

The two strays looked and nodded.

'Well, if you go up the down and then down the down on the other side, you'll see a meadow surrounded by trees. That's where it is.'

'Do you want to see our laboratories?' asked Atom.

'No thank you,' replied Clem remembering to be polite. 'We need to find Catrina, so we'll be off now.'

Chapter Nine

THE CONVENTION

As they descended down the down, they noticed a variety of animals in the distance sheltering beneath trees on the slopes of a valley. A disused railway track ran along the bottom of the valley parallel to a fast-flowing chalk stream.

An ageing donkey with three teeth missing and bad breath approached them. 'We are holding our annual convention,' he spluttered without introducing himself.

Jet and Clem stood back.

'It's the third year we've held one,' continued the donkey slowly. 'It was my idea in the first place. You see, I wanted to give something back to society in my twilight years.'

'What's a convention? asked Clem.

'It's an ass-embly, but not just for donkeys. All animals are welcome, so long as they don't fight each other or try to eat the lesser species. It is a peaceful gathering for animals who are prepared to live on a vegetarian diet for a couple of days. We have local tours and visits, exhibits, meetings, and conferences on all sorts of topics. Do you want to join us?'

'We are two strays,' said Jet. 'Clem is looking for his sister.'

'We might be able to help you in your purr-suit of your sister,' said the donkey.

'And pigs might fly,' whispered Clem to Jet. 'Don't get near him. His breath stinks of rotten straw.'

'Shush!' she replied covering her mouth so that the ass couldn't hear. 'Can't you see that the old donkey is trying to be nice to us and, don't forget, he says it's a peaceful gathering.'

'Is there an entry fee to join your animal assembly?' asked Jet anxiously.

'It's usually a guinea,' replied the donkey. 'But this year, our treasurers, the guinea pig and the guinea fowl, have kindly waived the registration fee. All you have to do is compose a sentence to illustrate how your family, in your case the cat family, have influenced the English language of humans.'

Jet and Clem followed the donkey along the railway track to several old railway carriages next to a field with a large pond. Animals large and small were milling around while others were swimming in the murky water.

'It's a bit like Noah's Ark,' remarked Jet.

The donkey led the two strays to a carriage with the words 'Registration Office for Smaller Animals' scratched on a window next to an open door.

Jet and Clem jumped into the carriage and headed straight for the registration desk. There was not an animal in sight. Clem pressed a bell on the desk. A parrot pounced onto the desk, stared at the two cats, and squawked:

> 'When the mussels tried to muscle their way in,
> The flies took flight.
> The scapegoats escaped,
> While the bees beat a retreat.
> The ants upped the ante,
> The bats went into battle but lost
> because they were batty.
> The ducks were bowled out for a duck.
> The hogs tried to hog all the food,
> But the dogs took it away in doggy bags.
> The fish thought that was fishy,
> Except for the red herrings who mislead them all.
> The owls howled.
> The sharks ripped everyone off.
> The spiders spied.
> The whales wailed.
> The worms wormed their way in uninvited,
> The rats ratified the deal but then became rattled,
> Because the foxes outfoxed them all.'

Jet and Clem listened in amazement as he continued to recite the lines animals attending the assembly had contributed.

'When, while, but, except, and because are all my words,' quipped the parrot. 'I added them. The rest are theirs. What do you have to offer?'

'That would let the cat out of the bag,' replied Jet cleverly.

'That would let the cat out of the bag,' parroted the parrot. 'Superb choice. I'll remember that. You may pass into the ass-embly.'

They walked through a couple of coupled carriages poking their noses into small gatherings looking for Catrina. But there was no sign of her. They talked to a few of the attendees who could speak English. 'Have you seen Catrina?' they kept on asking, but not one had.

'We'd better leave and head south,' suggested Clem. 'It's hopeless here and I've haven't seen one other cat.'

'Yet!' replied Jet. 'We haven't seen one other cat – yet! There's sure to be some of our kith and kin here. Let's try just one more meeting. You never know your luck. They entered another carriage where a conference for 'Our Colour-named Avian Breth-wren' was in full session.

Blue tits, yellow hammers, red kites, green finches, blackbirds, and snow owls flew around chirping and chasing one another. Some were purr-ched in the racks above the seats. A sign read: 'Remember – This is a vegetarian convention. Our conference is a non-meat-eating meeting. Please refrain from hunting and killing one another.'

'The snow owls shouldn't be here,' whispered a stocky cat who had just entered the carriage. The cat had thick greyish brown fur, spots on her head, and black rings on her tail. She had a cat-watch strapped to her front right leg, just above the paw.

'Snow owls don't have a colour in their name. But we decided to let it pass, as we don't have any white-named birds here. We did invite some whitethroats, but they couldn't make it. They sent their apologies.'

Jet held out a paw and wagged her tail in friendship. Clem cowered. He was suspicious. The three cats moved to a quiet area beneath a seat in the next carriage.

'My name is Manul,' said the cat. 'I'm a Pallas's cat and I've come all the way from Afghanistan.'

She explained that she was a refugee. She used to live with her family in complete safety in the mountains. But then she was caught by a human and put into a cage. After a long dusty journey on a horse, the cage was thrown into the back of a truck.

'They were taking me to a zoo in Europe where they could get a lot of money for me. But I escaped and jumped into a freight train wagon. When it stopped, I saw a big lorry being loaded with large wooden crates. I jumped in to hide. There were several humans in the lorry as well. I was there for many hours and I got increasingly cold, hungry, and frightened. I was worried the humans might spot me and try to eat me.

Eventually a man in a black uniform, a policeman I think, opened the door. I saw lots of lorries, vans, cars, and overflowing litter bins. It was a motorway service station. The driver joined the policeman as they looked around flashing their torches. Before they could see me, I leapt out and scampered across the tarmac. I stopped on the other side of the lorry park and gobbled up some scraps of food from the bins. After resting a bit beneath a white van, I wandered across fields, jumped across ditches and streams, and got lost in copses. I met several other cats as I passed through villages. They congratulated me on my command of English which I'd learnt while listening to the humans on my travels. The cats also told me about local customs. And then I heard the donkey beckoning to me - so here I am.'

Jet and Clem listened intently.

'I see you are domesti-cats with official stray collars,' continued Manul. 'I'm a wild cat but very friendly. When I met the donkey we talked about a human convention I'd seen in Afghanistan. It was called a jirga. He asked me if I could organise a similar meeting for animals visiting or residing in the downs. I jumped at the chance. That was over three years ago.'

'Are you in charge here?' asked Jet.

'Yes.'

'What do you do if animals start attacking one another?'

'We alert the crows. They immediately take flight and call on security. Our guard dogs are well-trained and do an excellent job, but they are always drinking water. We call them the "thirst responders". We then get the offenders together in our "carriage of quietness, meditation, mindfulness, and reflection" and ask our doves to talk to them about love, peace, and tranquility.'

'The convention does seem well organised,' said Jet trying to please the Pallas's cat.

'What is your specific interest here?' asked Manul. 'We have lots of meetings and opportunities at our convention for you and our other fellow travellers in the animal kingdom to engage peacefully with one another.'

Jet explained that they were hoping to find Clem's long-lost sister Catrina at the convention.

'So that's the purr-pose of your visit,' said Manul. 'Unfortunately no cat with that name has registered here. In fact, apart from the two of you, no other cats have registered. We are therefore delighted to see you, but I understand that you want to continue looking for her – and I may be able to assist you.'

She pointed out that she had arranged an excursion for cats to look at some of the science laboratories lo-cat-ed along the valley on the other side of the old railway station. 'As we are the only cats attending the convention, I can take you on the tour right now. You will be able to examine our breth-wren's impact on science. As you will see, cats are highly influential in science.'

'How will the laboratories help me to find Catrina?' asked Clem, forgetting that he had declined Molly Cool's offer of a visit.

Manul looked at Clem hesitantly. 'I was never good at science myself, so I don't know, but I'm confident the lab cats will be able to answer your question and point you in the right direction.'

'Let's go,' said Jet, ignoring Clem's reluctance.

Chapter Ten

THE LABORATORIES

Manul led them along a rusting railway track past the station and then along the chalk stream being careful to avoid human anglers who were fishing for trout. They came to a field littered with wrecked cars, old cabins, abandoned caravans, and a collection of delapidated mobile homes.

'The cabins and caravans are the catchemistry laboratories,' said Manul waving a paw at the field. She raised her front right paw and cast a glance at the cat-watch. 'Oh my gosh! I've just remembered I have a team meeting in ten minutes. I also need to keep an eye on the proceedings and activities at the convention. So, unfortunately, I'll have to leave you now. One of our cat breth-wren, I'm sure, will come out to meet you and show you around the laboratories.'

Jet and Clem noticed two cats in white coats having a smoke at the entrance to the one of the caravans. They instantly recognised them. It was Atom and Molly Cool. As soon as they saw the two strays, they stubbed the cigarettes out and wandered across.

'Hello again,' said Molly Cool. 'I see you've changed your mind. You won't regret it. Atom and I will be delighted to show you around our laboratories.'

Jet said she would love to have a look round. Clem was less keen. He was getting tired and anxious to move on in their purr-suit of Catrina. He couldn't imagine how catchemistry could help him find Catrina.

'Manul suggested you might be able to help us find Clem's sister Catrina,' said Jet.

Molly Cool winked. 'You can always trust a catchemist to find a solution. I'm looking forward to your reaction when you see what we do. We work here along with other catchemists in the purr-fume laboratory and I think I know just the purr-son for you.'

Clem was still not convinced. 'We have a few minutes for a quick look, but then we must move on,' he said grudgingly.

The two catchemists pulled out safety goggles from the pockets of their coats, put them on, and headed straight to the entrance of a ram-shackle caravan. Jet and Clem followed. Molly Cool handed the two strays white coats and safety goggles that were hanging on hooks inside the caravan.

'Please put these on,' she said. 'We take the health and safety of our staff and visitors very seriously. If you hear a fire alarm please exit immediately through the nearest door or window leaving all your possessions behind.'

'We don't have any possessions except our collars,' said Clem. 'You can leave those on.'

After Jet and Clem had put on their white coats and goggles, Molly Cool wren-ched open a drawer and extracted two sticky labels, each with the word 'VISITOR' on it. She pressed them onto the left-side lapels of their coats.

A creased poster on a wall inside the caravan showed an apple falling from a tree onto the head of a newt.

'This poster has an important message,' she explained. 'Although cats had a major impact on science, we must acknowledge that other animals also contributed. Isaac the Newt, for example, discovered the laws of motion that keep us all moving and the law of gravity which makes apples fall onto the ground instead of ascending into heaven.'

Another poster had lots of little squares with letters in them.

'That's a purr-iodic table. All the elements known to animal-kind are shown here. They are arranged in horizontal rows known as purr-iods. Each element has a sim-bull. As you will see, other animal families discovered many of the elements.'

Molly Cool pointed a paw to the square in the top left corner. 'The first sim-bull is H. Cows gave it that name because humans used to hide the element hydrogen inside their hides. The cows' cousins, the oxen, discovered ox-ygen, another element. They used it to make ox-ides.'

'The element has the sim-bull O for obvious reasons,' added Atom, indi-cat-ing a square in the top right of the table. 'The cow and the ox then got together and made hydroxides. Wasn't that clever?'

'But it was cats who first prepared purr-ox-ides,' continued Molly Cool enthusiastically. 'Humans use it to dye their hair white. They call them purr-ox-ide blondes. And did you know that pigs invented iron?'

'How come?' asked Jet.

'Haven't you heard of pig iron?' asked Atom condescendingly. 'And don't forget ants named the element antimony after they found it in the ground.'

Molly Cool moved her paw to the square on the left of the O square. 'That's N for nitrogen. Where do you think that came from?'

'Nits!' exclaimed Atom before the two strays had a chance to reply. 'And the tits discovered titanium.'

'Did seals give us silver?' asked Clem pretending to be interested.

'Hardly,' said Molly Cool. 'But another animal that lives on land and in water discovered another precious metal. It is related to us. Can you guess who it was?'

Jet and Clem looked at one another with puzzled expressions.

'No,' they said in unison.

'Platinum is named after the platy-puss,' said Molly Cool. 'Now I have an easy question. Which, or should I say what, precious metal was co-invented by the golden eagle, the goldfinch, and the goldcrest?'

'Gold,' replied Jet instantly.

'Exactly. And one final question.'

Molly Cool showed them a picture of a butterfly. Its wings were bright orange with black spots and a dark border. 'What, or should I say which, element did this butterfly alight on?'

Clem closed his eyes in thought. Jet gazed at the picture and then remembered. 'That's a copper butterfly,' she said.

Molly Cool patted her on the back and smiled. 'Yes, a common copper alighted on the metal many centuries ago.'

At that moment an ageing male cat with a dirty white coat climbed slowly up the steps into the caravan. He stood at the door breathing heavily. The two strays noticed his large belly and stern expression.

'He's eight kilos if he's an inch,' whispered Clem to Jet.

'You mustn't be rude to our hosts,' she replied quietly. 'And don't mix metric units with im-purr-ials, or confuse weight with length,'

Clem frowned, failing to understand what she meant. The fat cat approached the group. Atom wished him a good day and rushed out of the caravan claiming that he had an ex-purr-iment on the boil.

'May I introduce our chief catchemist, Boron,' said Molly Cool. 'Boron is head of all the laboratories on this site.'

The fat cat greeted the two visitors with a grunt and grubby pawshakes.

'Our chief always likes to say a few words of introduction to our visitors,' said Molly Cool, 'He will then show you around our laboratories.'

'Welcome to you both.' said the chief in a deep voice, squinting intently at Jet and Clem. 'I'm sure you will find much to interest you in our splendid laboratories. During my many lives, I have studied chemistry, practiced chemistry, and loved chemistry. Sadly, humans have now pushed us cats out of chemistry. But I'm proud to say that we have left our mark, or should I say, many marks. You can find them in the written words currently employed in the world of English-speaking humans. As you well know, the no-men-clature of cats has now coalesced into nomenclature. But, unlike the ubiquitous presence of cats in the human language, you find no men in most of the words used by humans.'

'He's men-tal,' grumbled Clem under his breath. 'You find men in cement, ailments, and torment.'

'Amen to that,' winked Jet.

Boron did not hear them. He pulled a small cotton cloth from his dirty coat and dabbed it onto his watery bloodshot eyes.

'It is well known that cats spend seventy-five purr-cent of their time sleeping. What do they do with the other twenty-five? Well, many of us embrace chemistry when we are awake. I speak as a catchemist who knows.'

Clem pressed his mouth up to Molly Cool's right ear and murmured. 'Did you say his name was Boring?'

Molly Cool took the hint. She clapped her paws, thanked the chief for his welcome and introduction, and suggested they all move on with the tour. 'Our two distinguished visitors have to hurry away on an important mission.'

The chief led them unsteadily down the steps of the caravan and clambered clumsily up the steps into a cabin. 'This is where Cat Alice, one of our catchemists, speeds up chemical reactions,' he croaked. 'Her group uses cat-alysts to cat-alyse reactions. We call it cat-alysis.'

'Will that speed up our search for Catrina?' asked Clem innocently.

'I don't think so,' replied Molly Cool. 'But one of our laboratories might be able to help. We'll get to that later, but first we must move on to another laboratory.'

They left Boron talking to himself and gazing vacantly at a rack of empty test tubes and a plate of ham sandwiches that Cat Alice had left on the bench for her lunch.

In the next laboratory, a spacious caravan, shelves were stacked with jars of powders and bottles of liquids. The benches were cluttered with pipettes, burettes, Bunsen burners, tongs, stands, clamps, spatulas, and other equipment.

'This is one of our busiest labs,' said Molly Cool.

She stopped next to a catchemist who was pouring a bright blue liquid from a conical flask into a glass beaker. An electric battery and two rods attached to wires lay on the bench. 'These rods are graphite electrodes,' he explained. 'One is called the cat-hode and the other the anode. The liquid is copper sulfate solution. When I put the rods into the solution, connect the wires to the battery, the cat-hode will look for copper cat-ions. And if we are lucky, we should get some bubbles of ox-ygen at the anode.'

'Isn't it wonderful what oxen, butterflies, and cats have discovered,' said Molly Cool. 'And now, for the final throw of the mice, let's move on to our olfactory section. It's our purr-fume lab. We are all so proud of it. Over the years we have achieved some fantastic results. We have won many awards for outstanding accomplishments.'

She explained that this was the laboratory that might help the two visitors to trace Catrina. Atom joined them from the other side of the laboratory where he had been clamping a burette onto a stand and using a pestle to grind a powder in a mortar.

'What does olfactory mean?' asked Clem whose curiosity had been sparked by the prospect of finding Catrina.

'It's to do with scent, purr-fume, aroma, fragrance, smell, odour, whiff, stink, or whatever you like to call it,' said a black and white cat who had just entered the caravan. Atom introduced him to the two strays. 'Boppin is the head of our purr-fume laboratory,' he said with a twinkle in his eye.

'Every cat has a unique smell profile,' explained Boppin. 'We call it the olfactory paw-print that purr-meates throughout the atmosphere and is carried on the breeze.'

He pointed out that no matter how careful a cat is in cleaning itself, it always carries the smell of its recent environment, whether it be the inside of a human's home reeking of pipe smoke and sweet tea, a garden full of fragrant roses and catnip, a pub smelling of beer, a field of new mown hay, or a forest of pines.

'Furr-thermore, we all emit hundreds of chemicals in every breath we exhale and we all release numerous chemicals from our fur and other parts of our bodies,' he said. 'Catchemical emissions that our breth-wren can recognise and respond to are known as furry-mones.'

'I can smell Clem from a mile off,' said Jet trying to make conversation. 'And his smell is so different from yours, Boppin.'

'Top professional olfactory catchemists like myself usually refer to the olfactory paw-print as an observable purr-fume profile or OPP for short,' said Boppin. 'Every family of cats has an intrinsic purr-fume profile which we dub IPP. The OPP, which is related to the IPP, is a characteristic that is unique for each cat. But it varies minute by minute, hour by hour, and from day to day. That's because it is modified by the cat's environment, its diet, its health, its hygiene, and whether it has been rolling in the grass, rubbing its nose with another cat, or sleeping near a road. We call this the modified observable purr-fume profile, or MOPP. It is a scientific term all expert olfactory catchemists like me understand.'

'This is getting very jargonistic and technical,' complained Clem who was becoming confused.

Boppin ignored his comment and continued. 'In our lab we can dismodify a cat's MOPP by removing the modifiers leaving the OPP, which of course, is gender and age specific and directly related to the IPP. We can never determine the IPP absolutely, except at birth.'

Atom noticed that Clem was not only unimpressed but also mystified.

'Boppin is also an expert obfus-cat-or,' whispered Atom into Clem's ear. 'He loves to hear his own voice and invent acronyms by the dozen just to confuse us.'

Molly Cool cast a glance at Atom and held a paw up to her mouth to signal to him to be quiet. Jet began to yawn. Boppin rang a bell. An athletic-looking white cat entered the caravan and sat down beside him. Boppin acknowledged the cat and resumed his talk.

'We receive MOPP samples around the clock from our regional cat investigators and their assistants. We convert these samples into OPPs, analyse them by gas catography, cat-egorise them by area, age, gender, and, if known, family. We then place them into specimen bottles. Each bottle is carefully labelled and kept in our sterile storage room which, of course, is refrigerated. Every OPP has a temperature-dependent half-life. So, each bottle we store has a sniff-by date. That depends on the chemical composition of the OPP.

'We also load all the data onto our secure database. I think you'll be impressed when I say that our current OPP database has over ten thousand cat profiles. The database enables us to find closely matched OPPs and even trail, track, and trace cats with similar OPPs. It's known as OPP trailing, tracking, and tracing. We can often relate an OPP directly to its IPP. And as the OPP is the major component of the MOPP, we can sometimes sniff our way to success. It is an essential feature of trailing, tracking, and tracing.'

Clem's eyes lit up.

'I will now hand you over to Nostril who is our senior analyst and trailer, tracker, and tracer,' said Boppin turning to the white cat. 'She can recognise all manner of IPPs, detect numerous OPPs, and mop up the MOPPs.'

Chapter Eleven

TRACKING THE SCENT

Jet, Molly Cool, and the white cat talked to one another quietly next to a bench in the purr-fume laboratory. 'I'm one of the top cat odour detectives in the country,' said Nostril pointing proudly to her flared nose.

Clem sat chatting with Atom on the other side of the bench. The catchemist told Clem in a low voice that colleagues in the laboratory were tired of hearing Nostril boast how she had won the regional sniffing championships three years running. 'She claims she can detect the merest whiff of a scent at distances of a mile or so. And what's more, she says she has the ability to memorise hundreds of smells. All hokum pokum, that's what I say. We've never been able to prove it because she refuses to be tested. But she does know her job – I'll give her that.'

Nostril wandered around the bench to join Atom and Clem.

'Are you ready?' she asked Clem.

'Ready for what?'

'I need to ask you a few questions before we proceed.'

Clem looked to Atom for reassurance. Atom gave him the claws-up indi-cat-ing that he should indeed proceed.

'When was the last time you saw Catrina? What was her age? Did she enjoy good health? What did she eat? Can you describe her?' she asked in quick succession.

Clem answered all the questions as best he could.

'Did you share a cushion or rug with her?'

'No, I usually slept in a basket while she slept on an armchair more often than not,' replied Clem.

'Did you rub up against each other?

'Of course, frequently.'

'Excellent. I now need to take a swab.'

She pulled a piece of cotton wool out of a packet and pressed it against the fur on his head and body.

'Paw me that, please,' she said gesticulating at an empty glass beaker on the bench.

Clem slid it along the bench to her.

She poured a clear liquid into the beaker and then dropped the swab into it.

'Paw me that, please,' she said stretching out a paw towards a glass rod.

She stirred the cotton wool and the liquid together and then filtered it through a filter paper and funnel into a conical flask.

'Paw me that, please' she said pointing to a specimen bottle.

After sniffing the flask, she decanted some of the contents into the bottle. Next, she added liquid from another bottle, screwed a plastic top onto the specimen bottle, and shook it furiously.

'That'll do,' she said holding it up to the light.

She carried it to a large machine with winking blue lights and a small screen resembling a computer monitor. The machine trembled and hummed expectantly as Nostril approached.

Atom, Molly Cool, Clem, and Jet sat and watched silently as she fiddled around with the machine for what seemed an eternity. Finally, she unscrewed the top of the specimen bottle and syringed some of its contents into the machine. She pressed a button.

'All done,' said Nostril.

She turned on a tap above a sink and washed her paws.

The blue lights on the machine flickered excitedly. A red light turned to green. After a while, spikey peaks appeared on the screen. They all waited as she twisted a knob, pressed some keys below the screen, and scrolled through lines and lines of words and numbers. The screen was too far away for Clem and Jet to read them. Eventually, she clapped her paws and shouted 'Eureka!'

'I have demodified your MOPP and you will be pleased to know that I have matched your OPP with a dismodified female MOPP specimen that arrived from Furthadown about a week ago.'

'What's the difference between demodified and dismodified?' asked Clem.

Nostril was about to reply, but Jet interrupted with another question: 'Where is Furthadown?'

'It's a small town near the coast – not far from here,' replied Nostril. 'It is famous for its fashion shows. Come with me – we should be able to find it and then track and trace Catrina's OPP trail.'

Atom, Molly Cool, Clem, Jet, and Nostril immediately took off their white coats and removed their goggles. They set out leaving behind the cabins, caravans, and the other animals now arriving for a tour of the laboratories.

Almost immediately they came to a bright yellow field of oil seed rape. The smell of the crop masked animal scents.

'We'll need to circumnavigate the field,' explained Nostril.

The quintet rushed around the field without putting their noses to the ground until they reached the other side. Nostril spotted a wooden stile and sniffed it. 'Can you recognise Clem's scent?' Nostril asked Atom, Jet, and Molly Cool.

'Definitely, it's one of the most distinctive smells I've ever come across,' Jet replied. Atom and Molly Cool nodded in agreement.

'And Clem, can you remember your sister's scent?' asked Nostril.

'I'll never forget it,' replied Clem.

'Magnifi-scent,' said Nostril, 'You and your sister's scent are very similar. Now smell the step on this stile. If that isn't the fresh OPP of Catrina, I don't know what is.'

Clem sniffed it and agreed. The others sniffed it and nodded their heads.

'Now, noses to the ground and let's see if we can find the fragrant Catrina.'

They wandered across a ploughed field to another stile where all five cats recognised Catrina's smell. The path led to Furthadown.

Clem was getting hungry and immediately detected a whiff of discarded hamburgers that had fallen from a waste bin at the back of a takeaway restaurant.

'It's a shame to leave them there,' he said.

They stopped behind the bin to feast on the rich pickings. Afterwards they pawed their way to a nearby stream, frightened away three mallard ducks, and lapped eagerly at the water to quench their thirsts.

After they had eaten and refreshed themselves, they resumed their hunt for Catrina. The five cats came to a shallow stream flowing rapidly over a road that led to the centre of Furthadown. They had no option but to wade across the ford. When they got to the other side, they stopped to dry their paws.

Clem put his nose to the road. 'We've lost her trail,' he said turning to Nostril. But she had rushed off ahead of them.

'I think it's Furrimagio,' she cried back them.

The four cats caught up with her. Nostril was staring at a slim and elegant Siamese cat with a patterned coat, neatly trimmed whiskers, long legs, and green eyes striding across the village square.

'Have you heard of Furrimagio?' Molly Cool asked the two strays.

Clem and Jet both shook their heads.

'She's the most famous cat fashion designer in the south,' explained Atom loudly. 'She's a real sophisti-cat.'

On hearing Atom, the fashion designer stopped, turned towards him and smiled.

'Smell the purr-fume,' she said.

The quintet held their noses in the air and sniffed.

'Jasmine,' announced Nostril knowingly.

'Exactly,' said Furrimagio. 'You can find it in lots of the gardens around here. It's one of my favourites. Now follow me.'

She pranced along with her head held high to a disused shed with a narrow carpet stretching from the entrance to the other end. Atom, Molly Cool, Clem, and Jet followed her not noticing that Nostril was no longer with them. They sat at the back near the entrance. Well-groomed cats of all shapes, sizes, and colours sat on either side of the cat-walk.

They could hear Furrimagio in a hidden part of the shed giving instructions to the models. Kitten after kitten looking gaunt and solemn paraded up and down the carpet to the accompaniment of rhythmic mew-sic wearing woolen hats, scarves, dark glasses, and shiny coats. The audience watched intently.

Clem felt a paw on his shoulder. It was Nostril. Her nose was twitching vigorously.

'She was here yesterday.'

'Who?'

'Your sister Catrina. I picked up her scent on the tree outside. She left a well-marked trail, but we must hurry. The wind is picking up and we don't want to lose her scent.'

The five cats dashed unceremoniously out of the fashion show.

Nostril, with nose to ground, dashed out of the town stopping frequently to sniff gates, fences, and trees. The other four cats hurried behind her and soon picked up Catrina's distinctive scent.

They sped past hedgerows, crossed roads, ran along public and purr-missive paw-paths, entered ancient woods, skipped and scuttled through fields of green wheat, and raced over fields to avoid grazing sheep and cows chewing their cud. The quintet eventually arrived at a shallow rivulet that trickled south through a gulley for several hundred metres before flowing into the sea. Nostril froze in her tracks.

'There,' she said pointing to a sandy beach in the distance. 'She'll be there somewhere. I'll go no further. If there's one thing I can't stand, it's sea water and the smell of seaweed.'

'That's two things,' said Clem im-purr-tinently.

'Even the sight of it makes me sick.'

'You get sea sick?'

'You have to get into a boat if you want to be sea sick,' explained Molly Cool. 'There is a word for her condition. It's marine aquaphobia.'

'That's two words,' said Clem.

Nostril turned round, bid goodbye to the other cats, and headed back towards Furthadown.

'Atom and I will go with her in case she needs help - and we have to get back to work,' said Molly Cool. 'Next time you're around here, come and visit us. It would be nice to see you again. I'm sure you'll find Catrina. Please bring her too. We'd love to meet her.'

Atom and Molly Cool chased after Nostril leaving Jet and Clem staring at one another.

'Where do we go now?' asked Clem.

'South to the sea, obviously,' grinned Jet.

Chapter Twelve

SOUTH TO THE SEA

The light was beginning to fade before they could reach the sea.

'We need to pawse before we venture fur-ther,' said Jet.

Clem agreed.

The two strays decided to settle down for the night. They found a bus shelter and snuggled down inside.

Jet awoke early in the morning feeling hungry. Clem snoozed. It was misty and still dark. A single-decker bus with just a couple of passengers passed without stopping. She decided to search for food and quietly strolled along the road until she came to a row of shops where a waste bin had been upturned. A mangy fox was scavenging amongst the bags, plastic bottles, and beer cans. Jet hunched down, pricked her ears, and bared her teeth angrily. The fox turned to look at her and wandered off nonchalantly.

She found an almost empty carton of milk and a juicy half-eaten chicken leg amongst the litter. After tipping over the carton and lapping up the last few drops of milk, she clasped the chicken leg between her front paws and knawed away at the flesh. The remnants of a tuna sandwich and a beef burger lay nearby. She put the sandwich and burger into a brown paper bag, gripped it with her teeth, and carried it back to the bus shelter as if it were a mouse she had caught.

Clem was waking up and stretching his legs. They ate the sandwich and burger and left the shelter.

'I can't see the sea, it's so misty,' said Clem. 'Which way do we go?'

'Like I told you before, the sun rises in the east,' said Jet pointing to a faint glow in the distance behind the shelter. 'We go down the road keeping the glow on the left.'

'And if it's not on the left?'

'We leave the road.'

The road descended and then curved to the right leaving the glow behind them. They jumped over a ditch away from the road and cut through a hedge into a field of short grass. The glow was on the left once again.

An early human jogger passed by without noticing them.

'I think this is a sports ground,' said Jet who could see the dark shape of a pavilion on her left.'

'It's darker on the right, so that must be west,' said Clem.

But the mist was getting worse and now they could hardly see fur-ther than their whiskers. They paw-sed for a while to take in breath and sniff the air.

After thirty minutes or so, the mist thinned momentarily revealing a bright light.

'Did you see that?' asked Jet.

'I saw the light, I saw the light,' replied Clem vaguely recalling a song he had heard on the radio before his home was flooded. 'No more darkness, no more night.'

The light reappeared and approached them gradually growing bigger as it did so. The mist swirled, congealed, and then engulfed the light forming a white cloud with a glistening silver lining.

Jet and Clem gasped in awe. They did not move a paw. The cloud floated over them and then slowly descended onto the grass about fifty metres in front of them. The cloud began to split into two halves that spread out like the wings of an angel. The wings floated away and dissolved in the mist. The two strays noticed something wriggling on the ground.

'It's a vision,' said Clem.

'It looks like an animal to me,' said Jet.

Clem sniffed as the animal approached. He pawed anxiously at his collar. The animal, the size of an adult cat, sparkled in the mist.

'I think it's one of our breth-wren,'

Jet took a few steps towards the animal, took a deep breath to draw in its scent, then leapt into the air.

'I don't believe it,' she screamed. 'It's Clawdia.'

The two strays rushed towards her. Jet and Clawdia rubbed up against one another, kissed each other on both cheeks, and purred joyfully. Clawdia was wearing a silver collar studded with purr-ls. Her claws were painted gold. Jet introduced her to Clem.

'After Jet told me that the two of you were heading south to the sea in search of Catrina, it occurred to me that I might be able to help,' said Clawdia. 'I thought to myself, it's nice to get out every so often, so why not chase after Jet and see if I can be of assistance. Mistress Maud is away on a cruise, you see. She left her neighbour Marjory to come in once a day to feed me. We have a cat-flap. I started out from Uppandown the day after Jet's visit and followed her vapour trail. I got as far as the Purr-haps family then lost her scent when it started to rain. But that didn't stop me. I decided to continue south through the down towns, villages, and farms looking for you.

'One cat I bumped into said he'd seen you heading to the intercounty strays' office. He spoke in a funny way, but I forget his name.'

'Do-it-tomorrow Tommo?' asked Jet.

'Yes, that's him. He said that after he had chatted with you, he'd seen Catrina near the History of the Cat Mewseum. Kingsley the kingfisher had a word with me at the lake and kindly offered to drop a line to Clem about the sighting. But I'm getting ahead of myself. Other cats I met after losing Jet's scent at the Purr-haps barn told me they had seen you both and, thankfully, paw-pointed me in the right direction.'

'Who did you meet?'

'Whom did I meet? Truffle Le Tracteur – he was so helpful, like all the cats in the county. They are so friendly. I'm so impressed. Purr-fectly Obvious: what a wise old cat. Purr C. Veer – he's so clever. Boppin at the lab – I didn't understand a word he said. He spoke in letters. Luckily your fellow travellers Molly Cool and Atom walked with me a little way. They were su-purr. And then I met Furrimagio. She just adored my collar and claws. "Oh darling," she said. "You must come to our next show." I told her I loved her purr-fume - jasmine I believe. Finally, I met Kingsley the kingfisher again. He worked his magic and brought me here. And now here I am, in seventh heaven. Guess what?'

'What?' asked Jet and Clem in unison.

'I've found Catrina!'

'Catrina, you've seen her? You know where she is?' asked Clem leaping in the air with excitement. 'How is she?'

'Enjoying a va-cat-ion by the sea, she told me. When she escaped from the flood, she searched for you but the waters had washed away all your scent. After several days of looking, she was exhausted and felt she needed a break. She came to the sea because she'd heard that the pickings at the seaside are excellent and there's lots of friendly company.'

'How can we find her in this mist?' asked Jet.

'It's a sea mist. The sun will soon burn it away and then we can look forward to a lovely warm day.'

The three cats sat cat-chatting until the mist cleared. As soon as they could see the sea, they hurried across the sports field, and raced along a human path that weaved through sand dunes. They came to a row of beach huts painted in pastel shades of blue, green, pink, and yellow. A promenade separated the huts from a sandy beach.

Clem turned to Clawdia. 'You didn't tell us where Catrina is. Are you sure you know where she is?'

'Of course, I know where she is, or least where she was when I met her. I saw her yesterday evening when I was walking along the beach looking for you. I thought you would have arrived by then. It was getting dark. Do you see those heavy wooden fences rising out of the sand and stretching over the beach into the sea?'

'What are they and why are they going into the sea?' asked Clem.

'They are called groynes. Humans put them in to protect the shore.'

'Did you see Catrina behind one?'

'Well, I was just about to jump over one of them yesterday evening as it was getting dark, when I stopped. There was a delicious smell of fish and chips, you see. I walked back up the beach to the promenade and the sea front shops. And then I saw her.'

'How did you know it was her?' asked Jet.

'Nostril had described her to me. She even allowed me to sniff a sample of her smell. I think she called it her OPP. Poor Nostril. She wasn't well – sea sick I think. She was so good to help me.'

Clem was growing impatient. 'Where is she now?'

'Nostril?'

'No Catrina.'

'Well, as I was about to say before you interrupted me, we cat-chatted for a few minutes. I told her that the two of you were looking for her and I was looking for you. She told me to tell you that she would wait for you on the beach tomorrow, that is today. I said I would find a warm place to sleep and work my Kingsley kingfisher magic to find you tomorrow, that is today.'

The three cats hurried towards the sandy beach. Human holiday makers and day trippers strolled along the sea front in droves. Ice cream licking youngsters wearing flip-flops and swimsuits lagged behind their parents. Elderly human couples rested in seafront shelters nibbling at sandwiches and pouring cups of coffee from their thermos flasks. Families thronged the beach sunning themselves on deck chairs or lying on towels under umbrellas. Children swarmed around with buckets and spades building sand castles. Others played ball games with one another.

The trio pawed their way slowly along the promenade in the shadow of the sea wall hoping not to be seen by the holiday makers. Jet darted at a pair of screaming seagulls and scared them away much to the delight of a group of noisy children.

A bronzed young man in bright green shorts and yellow T-shirt stopped and bent down to pet Jet. Clawdia whispered in her ear advising her to purr, raise her tail, rub against the man's leg, and then walk on. 'Don't let him pick you up. He might kidnap you and take you home.'

Jet thought about that. Clawdia had a good home to go to, so why shouldn't she have one to go to too. Maybe she should allow the young man to pick her up and stroke her. But the man didn't. He jumped up and chased after his children.

'You were lucky there,' said Clem. 'He could have cat-napped you.'

Clawdia had ambled on ahead of them. 'Where is Catrina?' he asked as the two strays caught up with her. She took them behind a beach café to avoid the promenaders and look for food. They found plenty of tasty morsels blown in from the overflowing litter bins. It was now late afternoon.

A small harbour came into view. A dozen or so sailing dinghies and yachts were anchored in the water. Others were tied up to the harbor walls. No more than a mile away, they could see an island with a ferry heading towards it.

The cats left the beach huts and seafront shelters and passed a small parade of shops and kiosks. They slowed up to search for Catrina.

Bathers and promenaders loaded with bags, towels, beach balls, and fishing nets were beginning to return to their cars. The cats decided to walk along the beach towards the harbour. Clem immediately recognised the rich sound of Catrina's purr and her distinctive scent. He tip-pawed towards a deck chair surrounded by collapsing sand castles. Clawdia and Jet followed.

'Let's surprise her!' he said.

Catrina was curled up on a towel that had been flung onto the deck chair. She was basking in the warmth of the setting sun. On hearing the approach of the three cats, she stretched out her legs and stood up. On seeing Clem, she sprang into the air ecstatically.

The brother and sister nuzzled one another and gazed unbelievingly into each other's eyes without so much as a purr. She explained that a friendly family had adopted her, with her purr-mission, for the afternoon. Her job was to look after the deck chair, towels, clothes, and picnic hamper while they were out bathing in the sea and walking along the beach.

Catrina took a hasty look at Jet and Clawdia and then sprinted away towards the harbour before Clem had a chance to introduce them. Clem waved a paw at the two of them and chased after Catrina.

'Wait here,' suggested Clawdia. 'They obviously want to spend some time together alone.'

The twins paw-sed and then wandered slowly to the harbour avoiding the families who had lingered to watch the sun as it sank in the west.

'The tide is turning,' said Clawdia. 'Some of the boats will sail out on the ebb tide to the island.'

On reaching the harbour they climbed up onto the harbour wall, but could not see Clem and Catrina. They hid behind a stack of empty lobster pots piled next to a rusty mooring bollard. After several minutes, they spied Clem and Catrina further along the wall. The brother and sister were cat-chatting to one another. Then, urged on by Catrina, Clem walked tentatively down a gangway onto a floating jetty where a sailing vessel was moored. Catrina shuffled along after him taking care not to slip or trip.

'Maybe they can smell fish in the boat?' suggested Jet.

Before the two sisters could blink, the skipper had cast off and the vessel sailed towards the harbour entrance. Clem and Catrina sat on the stern out of his sight. Clawdia and Jet rushed along to the far end of the wall. They waved their front paws vigorously at Clem and Catrina as the vessel passed by and out of the harbour. Clem saw them and, grinning from ear to ear, blew them a kiss.

'Where is it going?' asked Jet.

'To the island,' replied Clawdia.

'What sort of boat is it?'

'It's one of our own designs. A cat-amaran.'

Jet smiled. 'They sailed away on a cat-amaran.'

'They sailed away into the sunset on a cat-amaran.'

The two sisters look at one another fondly as they watched. When it had disappeared they returned to the sandy beach. All was now quiet as the sun sank behind the horizon.

'Let's settle down in a beach shelter for the night and then go home?' suggested Jet. 'And on the way, we could visit Molly Cool, Atom, and the gang …'

A noise stopped her mid-sentence. Faint at first and then louder and louder: clippity clop, clippity clop. They turned to see a black horse charging towards them neighing and swishing its mane and tail in the air. Its hooves kicked up clouds of sand. The two cats leapt over a groyne and landed up to their necks in water. They swam and splashed their way through the darkness. The horse jumped over the groyne appearing not to notice them. But then, before they could reach the shore and the flickering lights of the promenade, the horse turned and galloped back towards them: clippity clop, clippity clop. The sound grew thunderous.

I cried out with a loud miaow. The nightmare woke me in a sweat. But Mistress Maud did not hear. She was in the garden mowing the lawn, tending to her roses, chatting to her neighbours, and singing 'Come into the garden Maud.' I immediately recovered and began to paw away on the laptop in her study before I could fur-get my dream. When she came back a couple of hours later, she settled down in her favourite armchair in the lounge, I rushed out of the study and jumped onto her knee. She stroked me on the head, tickled my ears, rubbed my chin, and then gathered a ball of wool and two needles from a side table. As she knitted, I told her with a long quiet purr about my nightmare. She ignored me. I don't think she even listened. Well, that's humans for you. They just don't understand.

CAT-A-LOG

To cat a log
is quite a slog.
To cat a word
is more absurd.
To verb a cat
or cat a verb
is tremendously supurrb.
To noun a cat
or cat a noun
is highly thought of, on the down.
And though it may not seem,
this has been a long long dream
So, to cat a log story short,
this is the end of my report:

Acknowledgements

I'd like to express my thanks to my human mistress who taught me to read and write English. While sitting on her lap in her study I watched her regularly compose messages on her laptop. She thus unwittingly taught me how to type and use her computer. I soon found time to paw away to my heart's content when she was dozing in the lounge, gardening, or away at the shops or garden centre. If, by chance, I heard her coming towards the room as I was writing, I'd quickly save and hide my work in a secret folder, switch off the computer, curl up, close my eyes, and pretend to be asleep on the desk. I'd like to dedi-cat this book to my twin sister Jet, my friends, and my neighbours who visited me in the garden on numerous occasions to sample our catmint, chase pigeons and squirrels, and share the latest cat-vine mews with me. They were all truly inspirational. Finally, I'm grateful to Michael

Freemantle, the human author to whom I emailed the text of my story and who arranged for it to be published. I absolve him from blame for any nonsense that may have inadvertently crept into my account.

BV - #0113 - 130921 - C0 - 203/127/6 - PB - 9781914195396 - Matt Lamination